Ariadne Breylard

Autumn

Knights Dream

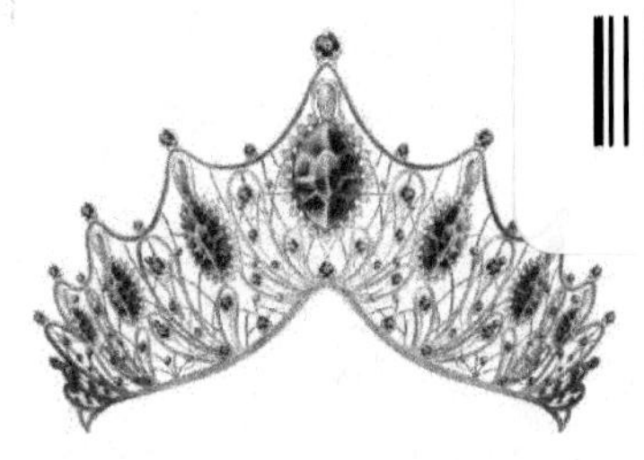

Editing by Madison Silvers

Proofing by Nina Fiegl

Cover art by Efa

Formatting by NVPLLC

Published by © Night Vision Publishing LLC (C1319203)

ISBN: PB: 978-1-963336-03-0

ISBN: 978-1-963336-20-7

Introduction

This Adult Fantasy Romance series is intended for mature audiences and is not suitable for young readers. The characters engage in multiple partner relationships and experience fated mates dynamics (why-choose). These relationships are inclusive, exploring diverse partnerships, including those of the same sex.

If themes such as LGBTQ+, multiple partners, open relationships, or poly are discomforting, it's advised to avoid this book series.

Themes and tropes in this book include: bonded, bullying, cliffhanger, enemies to lovers, fated mates, inst-love, love triangle, multiple POV, other-women-drama, second chance, secret identity, slow burn, smut/sexually graphic scenes with explicit language & description, soulmates, and steamy/suggestive scenes, unrequited love.

This book will end on a cliffhanger.

Ariadne Breylard

Autumn

Knights Dream

To the Stars
for letting me wish upon you

Contents

Chapter One

"How?" The warmth of my whisper clouded in the chilly air. The ice-blue gown I'd been wearing moments ago was now the black regal dress my reveal magic replaced it with, along with the subtle weight of my tiara, signifying I was no longer hidden by the geas.

The bond thrummed happily in my chest as I stared down at the gorgeous male. I was beyond ecstatic but hated that I was also worried something had gone wrong. He looked up at me with such focus his gaze felt heavy. As he knelt before me, he gently squeezed my hand and his deep voice filled the space. "The moment I saw you, everything else ceased to exist. Nothing and no one will ever be as important to me as you are. I realize that everything I have put myself through—the power I've gained, the trial of my patience, even the anger and resentment I've experienced toward magic and fate—have all served as tests, preparing me to deserve you. Regardless of your identity, our bond would have left me humbled. Though, now, I understand the purpose behind my prolonged wait. You are my Princess and will be my Queen, but you weren't ready for me yet."

"But I am now." I dropped to my knees, thankful for the billowy fabric cushioning my fall. From my position, I had to look up at him, but the way his eyes bore into mine, I didn't feel small.

Lifting his free hand, he ran the back of his fingers down my cheek, lowering his voice as he vowed, "I surrender myself to you—my allegiance, my devotion, and my love. Accept me as your Winter Knight, Lyra, so that I may prove my worthiness to you."

I wasn't surprised that he knew my name. I'd already guessed why he was with my parents when I came into the room—but it made me blush all the same.

"I accept you, and I accept our bond, Khade."

His eyes flashed, and the corner of his mouth tugged at the recognition. His name and face were well known, after all. How could I not know the infamous Queen's council, Khade Ranehall? He was nearly as famous as my mother, in the kingdom and inside the castle.

"You are my Winter Knight, now and always. Never bow to me again. You will stand beside me, never lower or higher. You are my mate, and we are equal in every regard."

Khade laced his fingers through my hair and held my head as he whispered over my lips, "So many surprises from you already, little mate, and we've only just met."

The kiss he gave me was just as brutish as the first, and it made me equally soften into him. Without breaking apart, he gripped me around the waist and stood with me in his arms before setting me on my feet again. He held me against him for a moment longer before releasing me.

"We have forever to get acquainted, but for now, your safety comes first." He swiped his thumb over my lips and took my hand. There was a thin, opaque ice dome around us that began to melt and vanish into thin air as our presence was revealed to the room.

Khade turned to look at me, then at the crown on my head, before focusing on my eyes. "Replace your glamour until we're secure," he ordered before turning to everyone.

It should have annoyed me to be bossed around like that, especially after just meeting, but it had the opposite effect and made me hot instead.

As soon as the ice was gone, our attention was drawn to the dark cover of my mother's shadow protecting the room. Every inch of the space surrounding my parents, brothers, and Vale was clouded with thick, black, liquid darkness, blocking and securing everything inside from potential witnesses. The only light in the room came from the portal Shea had created, and even that wasn't bright against the vacuum of my mother's power.

"Knight Ranehall," my mother greeted, acknowledging his new title for the first time.

"My Queen." Khade tipped his head forward in deference to her, then again to each of my fathers, before looking at the High Priestess. "It appears your services weren't needed after all." Khade lowered his gaze in respect.

"Perhaps." The High Priestess tucked her hands into her robe as she looked Khade and me over. "Or my presence was determined by fate."

My mother hummed. "I'm inclined to agree." She looked at the High Priestess, then the two women smiled at each other before facing us again. "It seems Lyra's fate beckons the unexpected."

The High Priestess's eyes crinkled with her obvious delight. "Mating bonds emerge in curious ways, but witnessing the reveal of a future queen is always replete with extraordinary wonder."

They both seemed at ease with everything, but every time I'd met one of my mates, it'd been unorthodox. "Why was the bond visible? The ceremony was over."

"My magic is still in the air, child. The spell to bring forth the bonds is powerful and lingers for a time." The High Priestess lifted a hand and swept it through the air, and her fingers sparkled. Tendrils stretched out as if seeking each bond in the room, but they became opaque, disappearing in the darkness before reaching anyone. "Even now, it's already receding, and so I shall take my leave." She swirled the little magic and brought it back into her. Then she winked at me, bowed to my mother, turned, and with a swift flick of her wrist, vanished through the wall.

Vale took his place by my side, looking me over as he took my free hand in his. “We need to go too,” he announced, then looked at Khade.

They simply nodded at each other, turned toward the portal, and each stepped forward to take the lead before coming to a halt to look at each other again.

I had to bite back a smile. Getting to know each of my mates was always going to be fun for me, but watching them adjust to each other would be wholly entertaining.

Chapter Two

Exiting the portal, I wasn't surprised to find that Shea had cast the spell directly into our family's dining hall. Once inside, Khade didn't pause or slow down as he pulled me along to the far side of the table, where my parents sat. My brothers and Roko followed through the portal last and took seats opposite us.

Khade released my hand to pull out a chair for me, then gestured for me to sit as he waited for Shea to banish the spell. The instant the portal was gone, he squared his shoulders and faced all five of my parents. "You'll have to forgive me while I process what's just happened. Let me start by addressing the geas contract and the information you provided me earlier—it's no longer sufficient. I require all the knowledge you have about Lyra, the threats made against her, every intelligence report, and all safety procedures you have in place." His words were firm and unyielding.

My father's voice rang loudly in the room. "I understand this is a shock for you, Khade—"

"It's more than a shock, Noel," Khade interrupted him. It took me by surprise to hear someone speak to my parents that way, but I didn't know their working relationship and hoped this was normal between them. "You can appreciate the situation, but there's more to this circumstance."

"You're upset, and in light of her revelation to you, we understand your furthered concern," Pai tried to assuage him, but Khade's demeanor didn't relax, and instead, the placation seemed to aggravate him more.

"Upset doesn't begin to cover it. I was upset while performing my duty for a hypothetical person. I was frustrated at having the hypothetical person and situations confirmed. Then, moments later, I discovered her as my mate. Now, I'm incensed. My mate has been here, under my nose, the entirety of my employ, and my duty to this kingdom and the role I've played until now feel predominantly inadequate."

Shea scoffed, drawing my attention from my winter mate to my winter brother. "She's just as protected today as she was yesterday." He drummed his fingers on the table. "Just because you're her mate doesn't change any of that, and just because this is new to you doesn't mean we've been slacking."

Khade looked down at my brother, but instead of scorn when he replied, his voice was as calm as it was cutting. "I too have protected her, but now that I'm fully involved, it wasn't enough."

"How?" Curiosity burned through me. Was it silly that the idea of him defending me before we met made me giddy? Probably.

Puck rolled his eyes at me. "He prosecuted cases." He smirked, then leaned forward and whispered as if we were alone and gossiping, "He even had a few of the offenders sent to the badlands." He waggled his brows as my eyes grew wide.

Had things really been that bad?

Khade turned my head away from my teasing brother and tipped my chin up to look at him. "It would have been my honor and duty to inform you of all the cases I worked on once you revealed yourself to the realm, but it was nothing you needed to worry about until then." His conviction calmed me, causing the sudden ball of nerves to disappear as quickly as it had come. He held my gaze with his unwavering one and gently stroked his thumb over my skin, only releasing and pulling away at the sound of my mother's voice.

"There are things you weren't meant to know yet, Lyra. Unfortunately, you two revealing to each other wasn't something that could have been foreseen or controlled." She gave me a weak smile as if apologizing for yet another inadvertent revelation of sensitive information I was learning before my time. "Now that you know about Khade's role, we can address any questions or worries you might have, but I assure you, there's no need for concern."

"Perhaps not from prosecuted cases of the past, but the present is indeterminate." Khade swiftly unbuttoned his suit jacket and slipped his hand into the pocket of his slacks. "The responsibility to keep her safe is more imperative now. I want to reevaluate the existing security measures and put in place additional safeguards, at the school and anywhere she spends her time outside of this castle."

"We trust your judgment, Khade. It was why you were initially brought into the fold. What more do you have in mind?" My mother acknowledged his request, opening up the topic for discussion.

He inclined his head, then seemed to steel himself for his first recommendation. "Thank you. I want to start with Araphel and expel the Spring noble from the academy."

"No." Father shook his head. "Absolutely not. We discussed this extensively, and the topic was settled."

"Which was the wrong decision then, and even more so now." Khade's voice dropped with the temperature in the room. "His actions were abhorrent under normal circumstances. He never should have been allowed to remain in attendance, and his proximity to her should have been forbidden."

"And your concerns and opinions were noted. However detestable Axel's actions were, ultimately his autonomy was recognized and determined non-punishable." Baba leaned forward, resting his forearms on the table. "You just learned that Lyra is your mate, so you are being given some leeway here, but you know we are doing everything within our power to keep her safe, keep her identity hidden, and staying vigilant against any and all threats to her and this kingdom."

"Leeway or not, Lyra's protection supersedes all my other considerations, as her safety is now my top priority," Khade asserted firmly; his voice was sharp as it cut through the air.

I stilled when he said this, but his expression remained neutral.

His top priority until an hour ago had been the Queen and the Realm. Khade and his family were staunch loyalists dating back to the first Queen, and while technically he was still on the side of the crown, he had just announced he was choosing me over the Kingdom ... and I didn't know how to feel about that.

Silence descended as the weight of his words settled like a heavy fog in the room. The magnitude of his declaration was undeniable, and I grappled with gratitude and uncertainty about how it would impact his role and our newfound connection. Though his words weren't treasonous, they clashed with the oath he had sworn to serve. Khade, along with every serving member of the Night Court, myself included, had promised to uphold the crown and, by proxy, my mother, above all others. With his statement, he was testing the boundaries of his allegiance.

My heart hammered as I glanced around the room and found my emotions mirrored in my brothers' expressions. Shock and disbelief were heavy, but with them was a flicker of understanding in their eyes. As the tension rose, we collectively held our breaths as we waited for my parents to respond.

After what felt like minutes but was probably only seconds, my father shifted and straightened in his seat before folding his hands in his lap, then looked at my mother. The ticking of the clock was loud as I braced myself and my thoughts threatened to spiral.

"With that statement, it's not a wonder why the geas revealed her to you so quickly."

"Your Majesty—"

"I'd already assumed as much"—my mother held up her hand—"and added with your service, I'm neither surprised nor offended. A summary of your remaining tests to put the room at ease will suffice."

Khade inclined his head before standing straight and pulling his shoulders back. "My unwavering acceptance was a test, but more so, it was my implicit and absolute loyalty to her even before we met. My lifetime of service to the crown was judged, but specifically, it was my unmitigated defense of her and dedication to her safety that were ultimately factored in. My humility and self-awareness were evaluated. And as you know, some of my tests will be ongoing. For instance, I recognized that, being Lyra's mate, there will be circumstances outside of my control. I had to acknowledge that and accept flexibility. With my trust in magic and fate, it was enough to satisfy the geas."

"Yes, you will face many tests—all of you." She looked from him to me, then to Vale, before allowing a smile to touch her lips. Her silent approval eased some of the pressure in the room as she briefly connected with each of my brothers and dads before focusing on my father.

My shoulders slumped with the pass Khade was given, and my brothers' audible sighs filled the otherwise quiet space, but the air still felt thick with tension.

"Your commitment to your duty and the crown will never cease to amaze me, Khade." Father raised a brow before returning to the original topic. "But you'll need to compromise on the matter of Axel. The situation has been settled, and change is not up for discussion."

"His father is likely the leader of the traitorous New Night Coalition. He can't be trusted." Khade steepled his fingers on the table and leaned forward. "The stakes are too high."

"No one is trusting him with anything." Papa shook his head.

"You're trusting her safety in his proximity." Khade turned steely eyes to stare him down. "They eat together, attend classes together, and share assignments." His voice had remained virtually neutral until he sneered at the last part.

"You're splitting hairs, Khade," Pai told him.

"Splitting hairs is what got her into this situation in the first place. The earthquake didn't care about your distinctions. What makes you think Axel or his wretched father will?"

"You're getting dangerously close to crossing a line, Councilor." My mother folded her hands in her lap, pinning him with a steely gaze. "Your concern for her safety and unwavering loyalty to Lyra have been made perfectly clear. However, the implications that this family and court are failing her will not be tolerated."

"My apologies, Your Majesty." Khade straightened and inclined his head to her. "I was only trying—"

"I know what you're trying to do, and as her mother, your defense and desired protection of her warm my heart," she said as her breath fogged in the room. "But as your Queen, I will remind you..."

My mother continued to speak to Khade as I wrung my hands together. They were clammy even as the temperature in the room plummeted again as the familiar bite of winter stung my nose.

"How are you, Princess?" Vale pulled my hands apart and smirked as he brought them to his mouth for a kiss.

I wanted to answer but couldn't find the words, so instead, I gave him a small smile as I tried to focus on him and the room around me. My chest felt tight as my heart raced, and even though it was cool in the room, I felt warm.

"Would you like something to drink?" Vale asked, distracting me as he peppered kisses over my knuckles, warming my icy hands between his warm ones. His familiar comfort allowed me to breathe a little easier.

"You're not considering the position it will put us in," Baba said, bringing some of my focus to them again.

"I understand that," Khade said as he reached forward and lifted the decanter of water that sat in the middle of the table in front of us. Next to it were glasses, a teapot with mugs, and snacks near a stack of small plates and silverware. It was an odd thing to notice suddenly, but Khade's movement and Vale's words brought my attention to it.

"To go back on that now could draw suspicion." Pai shook his head.

"I'm simply suggesting we discuss it again and consider alternative options," Khade argued as he poured a glass of water and, to my surprise, set it in front of me.

"Just because your opinion changed?" Shea scoffed. "Ridiculous."

"Yes." The decanter thudded against the table when Khade sat it back down. "That's what happens when new information comes to light. Perspectives evolve."

Shea crossed his arms and shook his head. "You're such a pompous ass."

"Don't make inane comments, then," Khade dismissed him with the remark, turning away from my brother and back to my parents.

"We can't just flip-flop on the decision without cause." Shea sat up straighter, glaring at Khade. He didn't like to be dismissed, regardless of the topic, but Shea's role in court made this doubly personal, especially since Khade's argument essentially questioned his professional responsibilities as an Intelligence Operator. "It makes us look indecisive and weak."

"And what message does allowing him to stay and get away with it send?"

"Keep your enemies closer—"

"Ugh, here we go." Puck groaned, thumping his head against the back of the chair.

"Yeah, this is getting sideways." Cleon rubbed his forehead.

"Agreed." Tunder knocked on the table. "I have a mate to get home to. Can we get back to—"

"Maybe you should try it sometime instead of resorting to—"

"We need to be adaptable—"

"And suddenly you're the expert on—"

There was so much going on I wasn't sure where to look, but when Vale's lips tipped up into a smile against my skin, I focused on him again.

"Would you like ice?"

I stared at him for a moment because I didn't get it. "What?"

"For your water." His eyes sparkled with mischief, but his teasing was lost on me.

My face scrunched with confusion. But then Khade's hand moved to hover over my glass as he countered Shea's arguments and tried to convince my parents to reconsider Axel's attendance. I watched as the rim frosted over before three perfectly square cubes buoyed in the liquid a moment later.

Khade's fingers flexed as his new demands were voiced. "Fine. Then place undercover guards in each of the classes they share, and no more partner assignments."

Vale's smile broadened. He didn't like my assignments with Axel either, so I thought he was reacting to Khade, but watching him closer, he wasn't paying attention to what they were saying, just what Khade was doing.

"We've considered that as well." My mother's tone was friendlier than the last time she'd spoken, and with my scattered focus, it was clear I was missing parts of the conversation. "That information will be in the reports you've requested."

"You haven't eaten in a while. Are you hungry?" Vale kissed my cheek. "There are some blueberries..."

Beside me, Khade grabbed a dessert bowl and scooped some of the fruit in. "And the partner assignments? What about those?" he repeated the question.

Puck snickered across the table, but I was too confused by Vale and his odd behavior to look at my brother.

"Perhaps it would be best if you read through all the information, and then we can discuss..." Baba was telling Khade, who sprinkled sugar on the berries after Vale had suggested it.

"You like them partially frozen, don't you?" Vale said to me, but his eyes were focused on the treat that Khade placed next to my ice water.

Khade's hand wafted over the berries. "And with chocolate." Khade took a few squares from the serving tray and placed them next to the berries. "I want all the information tonight," he said, then opened a napkin, stopped, and turned to look down at Vale. "Is this how you want our introduction to go?" he asked, and I finally understood that Vale had been misdirecting me to distraction.

Vale shrugged and ran his fingers across my neck. "You're freaking out our mate. I'm just keeping things casual while you settle in." He raised a brow at him, not hiding his smile as he leaned forward and kissed my temple.

Khade squatted beside me, and turned my head to look at him. He said nothing, instead searching my face for a moment before sighing. When he stood, he bent and kissed my forehead before turning to my family again. "It's been a long day. The rest of this conversation can wait until I've read through the reports."

"Thank you." Puck threw his arms up. "Can we go now?" He didn't wait for an answer before he took Roko's hand and stood, pulling his mate up with him.

"Just one last thing." Khade buttoned his suit jacket. "I'm going to jump to conclusions and assume that I'll be the concealed mate." He didn't frame it as a question but rather a statement. It was something I hadn't considered until he brought it up. And it didn't really require an answer. We all already knew, but there was a noticeable pause in the room anyway.

"Yes," Baba confirmed. "It would seem that the magic has chosen you for that task."

Suddenly, it didn't seem fair that I had revealed to him privately, and I felt a pang of sympathy for the burden. The Queens of the kingdoms were the only fae to have four or more fated mates—a widely acknowledged fact. Because of this, the geas that bound us was designed to select one of the first three mates to remain concealed until the final mate was accepted and the concealment magic was lifted.

Khade nodded, and though I'd expected him to be discontented about it, based on his actions leading up to this moment, I was surprised to find something else in his eyes when he looked back at me.

"I've waited for you this long publicly. It seems fitting I should get to keep you privately for a time." He smirked, then his pupils narrowed into slits as his shifted form made a subtle appearance.

Chapter Three

My brothers left quickly after being granted permission from my parents to do so. Even Puck, who would typically stick around to be nosy, fled the scene with Roko in tow. The entire week leading up to the Winter Revelry had been an emotional rollercoaster, and the whole day I'd been a ball of nerves, but I wasn't alone in my trepidation. I knew my family was also experiencing stress, so I couldn't blame them for taking their leave so eagerly.

"You're welcome to stay," my mother told me after releasing me from a hug. "Your things have been moved to your new mated suite."

"Thank you." I tried not to blush, but how exactly did someone control the flow of their own blood?

"Of course, my darling." She winked. "Vale, Khade, our home is yours. You're welcome to furnish your private quarters with your belongings and stay anytime you wish. It's always a pleasure to see you, Vale." She smiled.

"Thank you, Your Majesty."

"Khade." She turned to him and lifted a brow. "I wasn't able to express my congratulations before."

Khade pinched his lips in contrition, placed a hand over his chest, and tipped his head. "My apologies for being overbearing. I will acclimate quickly."

"I'm sure you will." She smirked at him. "I couldn't be more pleased to welcome you into our family."

"Thank you." His features softened when he looked at me, changing from his resting stoic expression to one of warmth. "There aren't words adequate enough to express how I'm feeling at the moment."

If I hadn't been blushing before, I certainly was now. I even felt flushed.

"I doubt that will stay the case for long." My mother chuckled as she ran a finger over my cheek. "I'm grateful she's found you, but even though she's my daughter, the kingdom's demands of you as my council remain the same."

Khade smirked. "I'd expect nothing less."

"In other words, no nepotism." Pai winked at me as he wrapped his arm around her waist. "For now, Vale and Lyra get a pass from royal duties, but you, sir, have a full schedule."

"More so now," Khade agreed, looking at me again.

We finished our goodbyes, and when we were alone, Vale wrapped me up in his arms. "Should we go home? Or do you want to stay here?" He kissed the top of my head before pulling back to look at me.

I looked at him and then at Khade. "I..." I shrugged.

Khade stepped forward, curling his finger under my chin. "It's been a long day. Perhaps you'll be more comfortable in your dorm rather than a new room tonight?"

"You'll come with?" I blurted, then bit my lip before I could say anything else that would make me feel silly.

He gave me a soft smile and leaned in closer. "Leaving you was never an option." He kissed the tip of my nose and looked at Vale. "Lead the way."

It was the middle of the night when we stepped through the portal and into the secret alcove outside of Araphel's entrance gates.

When Vale took my hand to leave the room, I stopped him to face Khade. "Do you have a glamour spell? You can't be seen." My voice raised with the realization of how unprepared we were. It should have been something we'd considered before the revelry and then again after, once I revealed to him, but with the excitement of the night, it had never crossed my mind until now.

The rush of nervous energy at the thought of getting caught—or worse, him deciding to leave and not join me—made my pulse race. "Maybe we should go back to the castle until we can figure something out."

Khade ran his hand down my arm, lacing our fingers together. The contact instantly calmed me. "I'll follow you my way." He lifted my hand, pressing cool lips against my skin briefly before releasing me. Then, he placed his hand on the small of my back and ushered me out of the room, with Vale leading the way.

When we reached the outdoors, Khade headed in the opposite direction of the entry gates than Vale and I were going. Just before we crossed through the concealment boundary that hid the alcove, I watched as Khade transformed into his massive Beithir serpent form. The shifting of his form was quicker than a wink, and if you weren't watching, you would miss it. Khade's Beithir serpent was an enormous and formidable creature. Beithir shifters were known for their swiftness and strength, and their venomous tails were both revered and feared.

Khade's form stood out even among his kind because of the unique traits he'd inherited from each of his parents. His massive viper head, with the addition of a cobra's hood, made him even more intimidating. He had a long, muscular body covered in black scales, which allowed him to blend seamlessly into the mossy forest backdrop. His eyes, which were a deep shade of purple, held a faint glimmer designed to captivate one's attention and divert it from the deadly touch of his venomous tail.

As he moved gracefully through the night, moonlight reflected off his obsidian scales, creating an ethereal glimmer that added to the mystique of his form. Khade's serpent shape was nearly unseen against the darkness, a creature of shadow that called to my own. My wings tingled with the denial of release, and watching him as he enjoyed the night, I made the decision that we'd need to shift together soon.

I'd only seen his creature form in PR photos and had never encountered another like him, so I couldn't help but stare with fascination as he slipped away, disappearing into the dense brush of the forest and trees.

It was quiet on campus, but Vale and I weren't the only ones making our way back to our rooms. We passed single students and couples still dressed in their evening finery, just as we were. There were also those wearing more casual attire typical of local festivals. I didn't begrudge my station or the requirements that came with it, but I was curious about what a mating festival looked like compared to the revelries I'd been to.

As we walked to our room, no one paid us any attention, although my hyperawareness was fixated on them. With Khade creeping through the woods to sneak into my dorm, I felt like a teenager smuggling a boy into my room. Scanning each of their faces, I searched for any sign of knowledge about what was happening under their noses, but I was only met with a cursory glance or smile in return.

"How are you feeling about everything?" Vale cast a privacy spell and then wrapped his arm around my shoulders, pulling me gently against his side.

"Anxious," I admitted, looking up at him before resting my head on his chest. "Everything is happening so fast."

"Nothing has to happen until you're ready." He hugged me tighter. "You were excited earlier. What changed?"

I shrugged. "Nothing's changed, really, but I didn't expect to reveal so quickly. And I feel terrible that he has to hide."

He chuckled and kissed the top of my head. "I wouldn't worry about that."

"Why?" I turned to face him again, a little surprised by the answer.

"Being the secret mate has its own perks. If I wasn't your first, I would have loved to be your secret." He whirled me around and playfully growled as he buried his face in my neck. "I'm a little jealous of all the fun you two will be having."

I giggled and pushed away from his pawing at me. "I don't know what you mean."

"Not yet, but you will." Vale bent down and kissed me in his fiery, possessive way. When I was breathless and aching for more, he released me. "We should get to our room, where I'm certain your serpent shifter is very impatiently waiting for you."

Since my senses were dulled from the geas and Khade and I hadn't completed the bond, I couldn't feel him yet. But I knew Vale could, and he'd likely been tracking Khade's movement the entire time. They were both predator shifters, and the ability was innate to their creature form. Plus, they both seemed to have that alpha, bossy possessiveness and were probably constantly assessing the other, even if they were doing it subconsciously.

We were almost at our building when that strange, creeping feeling came over me again. A gentle prickling sensation traveled up my neck as warmth spread down my arms and back.

I put my hand on Vale's chest and tugged at his shirt slightly to get his attention. "Do you feel that?" Even though his privacy spell was still up, I whispered to him.

Bending down, he buried his face in my hair. "No. I don't feel anything. I'm going to drop the spell."

But it didn't matter. The sensation was gone as quickly as it'd come, and if there had been anyone or anything for him to pick up on, it wasn't there any longer.

"Maybe I'm just tired," I told him when we were inside. "It's been a long night."

"Maybe. But we're not going to ignore anything—" He paused mid-sentence to look down at his phone when a message interrupted him with a ping. "Hm." He squinted at the text.

"Who is it?" I asked, flicking on the lights once we were inside ... and then sucked in a startled breath as the answer stood on the balcony. "Axel." I gasped.

"Son of a bitch." Vale slammed the front door behind him before marching forward and wrenching open the glass door. "I told you not to fucking come here." He shoved his finger into Axel's chest.

But Axel wasn't paying attention to his angry friend; he was just staring at me, his eyes roaming over the icy blue gown I was wearing.

"You look so beautiful, Lyra." His voice was quiet in the silence of the night, but I heard it as loudly as if he were saying it at full volume right next to me.

Vale dropped his head, pinching the bridge of his nose. "What do you want, man? It's been a long night." He huffed, sounding as exhausted as I knew he was pretending to be.

Axel didn't respond and instead kept his intense focus on me as he roamed his eyes over my features, capturing me in his heavy gaze.

After all the excitement of the night, meeting another mate and revealing to Khade, having the one who had rejected me stare at me as if I were his air to breathe was nearly overwhelming. My breathing sped up as the tension grew, and the longer the silence remained, the faster my heart beat in my chest. It was cruel, in a way, almost like salt in a wound—one I knew wouldn't ever fully heal but hadn't realized was still raw and open.

Axel took a step forward and lifted his hand as if to reach out for me, but was stopped by Vale. The thump of his hand as he smacked it against Axel's chest made him wince.

"What are you doing here?" Vale's voice was lower and less friendly this time.

Axel's eyes widened as he mumbled, "I... Sorry. I just needed to know..." He rubbed the heel of his palm against his breastbone and shook his head as if he were in a daze. "I-I ... wanted to make sure there weren't any problems," he stammered before looking away from me and up to Vale. "From my father." He sneered as his features hardened. Then he gritted his teeth and ran a rough hand through his hair. He stumbled a step back and yanked on the dark blond roots, looking distressed. "I'm sorry. I shouldn't have come."

I didn't know what it cost him to defy his father and stay away from the revelry, but he had, and for that reason alone, I felt indebted to him.

"Everything was fine, Axel." The swish of my gown sweeping across the floor brought his attention back to me. He was obviously frazzled; his eyes even looked wild. "Nothing to be concerned about happened."

He pulled in a breath so deep his chest noticeably expanded from the intake. It was only after he released it that his eyes softened. "Good. That's... I'm glad." His lips lifted in the tiniest smile. "Was there... Did you meet—"

"Listen, we just got home. It's been a long night," Vale interrupted, pulling me closer to him.

"Yeah, of course. No worries." Axel raised his hands and took a few steps back. "Sorry, I didn't mean to intrude. I..." He shook his head and turned for the stairs. "Sorry. Have a good night."

I reached out to get Vale's attention and tipped my head toward Axel's retreating form. *Go,* I mouthed to him. We proceeded to have a silent conversation before he relented.

"Axel. Wait," Vale called out. "Give me a few, and I'll swing by."

Axel spun around with a wrinkle in his brow. "What? But I thought—"

"Lyra's tired, but I could use a drink if you're up for it?"

"Yeah, but—"

"I'll lock up and be right behind you," Vale told him, not taking no for an answer.

Before Axel could say anything more, Vale and I were back inside, and he was closing the door as if to lock up for the night. Axel didn't linger.

A few minutes later, after encouraging Vale and reassuring him it was a good idea to go, Khade walked through the sliding glass door—calm, confident, and thoroughly unimpressed.

"Does he do that often?" he asked, unrushed in tone, though there was a bite to his words.

"No," I told him, watching him lock the door and pull closed the heavy curtains. "He's never done that before."

Khade turned around, his features softening a touch when he looked at me. Then he looked at Vale and raised a brow.

Vale tossed his jacket on the chair, followed by his vest and tie. "Since there's no sense in lying to you, yes. He's been here, but I wouldn't call it often," he grumbled, crossing his arms over his chest.

"What?" I spun to face him. "When? Why?"

Vale's irritation leeched away with a sigh. "It's only happened a few times. It seemed best to handle it quietly." His shoulders slumped when he looked at me, and his voice became a mix of reluctance and concern.

"A few times?" My throat seemed to dry at the words.

Vale stepped forward and wrapped his large hands around my face, ducking down to look directly at me. "I didn't want you to feel uneasy, so I didn't tell you. I should have, but I was trying to protect your sanctuary."

"I wish you had."

"I would never keep anything from you if I thought it jeopardized your safety. You know that, right?" His brow furrowed, but he wasn't asking for assurance, just confirmation in the trust we shared.

"Yes." I relaxed against him, winding my arms around his waist. I couldn't fault him for wanting to protect me from unnecessary worries, especially when it came to Axel.

"I know not everyone agrees, but I don't think Axel's a threat to you." Vale kissed my forehead and then released me to look pointedly at Khade. "There are spells on this building, and her brothers made a sibling pact with her. If not for those, my complete faith in that magic, and my belief he would never harm her, I wouldn't have had to sound the alarm because I would have taken care of him myself." His voice lowered into a rumble toward the end of his tirade.

Khade had kept a stern focus on Vale as he'd spoken and held his silence for a moment before easing his tense stance. "I detected the spells. But tell me about the pact," he pressed on, though his tone was less scathing. As he waited for Vale to answer him, he draped his suit jacket over the back of a dining room chair before unbuttoning the cuffs of his shirt to methodically roll up each sleeve. His long fingers moved swiftly, first with the cufflinks and then with each fold, until they were resting casually under his elbow. His arms were lean muscle with dark hair, and it took four folds before they were in place.

My mouth went dry as Vale told him about the sibling pact while I not-so-subtly ogled my winter mate. He moved closer to me in the process, and when Vale was done explaining how my brothers tricked me, Khade put his finger under my chin to meet my eyes.

"You have council now, my mate. Perhaps we should revisit the topic and perform a mate pact." He smirked at me, and the way his eyes roved over my face, I knew he was taking in my blush.

"I ... don't ... uh ..."

Vale chuckled, interrupting my stuttering with a peck on my cheek. "I'll be back in a couple of hours. I'm sure you'll hardly even notice I'm gone." He winked. When he reached the door, he turned and nodded at Khade. "Lyra's gown is tricky. She'll need help to get out of it." A beaming smile stretched across his face before he shut the door behind him.

My eyes widened at the insinuation, and I swore I heard his laugh echo down the hallway. "He's teasing me." I looked up at Khade.

"Yes, he's an instigator. I've already figured him out, though it wasn't hard," Khade remarked with a wry grin before crushing his mouth to mine.

I chirped in surprise but melted into his hold. He pulled me against him, pinning my body to his with one arm while his other hand slipped up the back of my neck to cradle my head as he held me in place.

He tasted like cold air on a snowy day, and even though his breath was cool, I felt warm in his arms. Khade's kisses were thorough and expert. He knew what he wanted and didn't seek to ask; he took what was freely offered with demand and gusto.

I was breathless and panting when he finally moved his lips from mine to run them along my jaw. The trail of his mouth and tongue along the sensitive skin sent chills down my spine that traveled over my body and perked my nipples at the tingling sensation.

Tipping my head back once he reached my ear, he kissed and bit down the length of my neck. My hands were pinned between us, and I could only fist his shirt as I moaned like a wanton, breathing heavily as my panties grew wet and my clit throbbed in time with my heartbeat.

Khade groaned with my mewling and tightened his hold on me, pressing his erection into my stomach when he took my mouth. When he released me again, he spun me around, then tipped my head to the side to kiss behind my ear.

"I want you, Lyra." He punctuated his statement by grinding his hardness into me again. "You smell like my every wish and desire come true, and when I take you, you're going to atone for the years I've had to wait to have you."

My core clenched at his words. I should have been alarmed, but I heard the stories and though I'd never been tied up for pleasure before, I was more than curious. Especially with him as my mate.

"Do you understand?" he demanded after pulling my earlobe through his teeth.

"Yes," I whined and squeezed my thighs together.

"You're not at fault for my suffering, but you, my love, are beholden to it. Am I making myself clear?"

I nodded.

"Use your words, Lyra." He tightened his hold on the root of my hair while nipping at my neck—neither of which was painful.

"Yes," I moaned in a whisper.

Khade pressed his lips against my throat in a firm kiss. "Good girl," he said, and I nearly came.

When he released my hair, he spread his fingers over my scalp and massaged my head as he unzipped my dress. Sliding the zipper down slowly, he slipped his fingers between the fabric of my gown and my skin, running the back of his knuckles down the length of my spine with his cool touch.

"When I make you mine Lyra, you will know me. We will rush nothing. You will feel comfortable with me and understand me as an individual and as your mate. When I have you, there will be no question of my loyalty or dedication to you. There will be no doubt of what you mean to me."

When my dress was loose and barely staying on my body, he languorously ran his finger back up my spine as he spoke. "When I fuck you, there will be no uncertainty of my devotion to you, and you will know it is not the bond pushing us together but the trust we've established and the emotional intimacy we share." He kissed my shoulder, then ran his nose up my neck to whisper in my ear, "Do you understand?" He pressed feather-light kisses down my jaw, wrapping his arms around my waist to pull me against him.

"Yes." I quivered in his embrace.

"Good." He pressed his hardness against me again. "Now, go change out of this gown and return to me in something comfortable, so we can talk."

Chapter Four

After hanging the dress, I washed my face, combed through my hair, put pajamas on, then hesitated at my bedroom door with my hand on the handle as I tried to reason with myself to stop stalling.

Khade was my mate.

I trusted fate again, and Vale had completely restored my faith in mate magic. I wasn't nervous about the bond, not really. My sudden reveal had been a surprise, but that's not what was making me anxious.

I was nervous about him being a whole-ass adult compared to my barely legal drinking age and recent introduction to society.

He had a career. A mortgage. He paid taxes.

I'd never even had a job.

What if I wasn't enough? Or too young and childish? I still laughed at Puck's goofy jokes and braided Callie's hair while we gossiped about boys over caramel drizzled ice cream.

He'd held press conferences.

I'd been at a kegger last weekend.

Sliding down the wall, I dropped my head between my legs, breathing through the creeping anxiety growing up from my belly and into my chest. I wasn't having a panic attack; this was a different type of inadequacy I was feeling compared to how I felt after Axel.

Then, I'd felt like trash; now, I just felt overwhelmed and underprepared.

I also understood that I was largely overthinking everything, but here we were and I was who I was.

Pushing my fingers through my hair, I held my head steady while I inhaled deeply through my nose, exhaled slowly between my lips, and tried to count myself up to move from the floor. I got to three, five times, when my phone pinged on the side table by the bed.

So instead of acting like the mature adult I was supposed to be, I embraced the drama, crawled across the carpet, snatched my phone off the nightstand, and sprawled out to check the message.

Vale: You're perfect.

That's all Vale had sent, but it was enough to make me smile at him and roll my eyes at my theatrics to get me off the floor.

Before I could second-guess myself again, I marched to the door, flung it open, and walked down the hallway to my living room.

Khade was sitting on the sofa like a dream plucked from my fantasies and made real. His eyes met mine, and with it was that smirk that lifted the corner of his lips and melted me on the inside. He was entirely too attractive to be sitting there, looking like he did, in my tiny academy dorm. He belonged on the cover of a magazine or a poster on my teenage bedroom wall.

His leg was bent over the other, and perched on his knee was a glass of some cheap booze not refined enough for him to put to his lips. His shirt was still tucked in but unbuttoned at the top, revealing a dusting of dark hair that had my imagination running rampant. His sleeves were bunched and tight around the muscles of his arms, and the way he was angled and staring me down reminded me of the men on the covers of those smutty romance books Puck and Roko liked to read.

Khade quirked a brow at me as I slowed my pace, then patted the empty spot next to him before draping his arm over the back of the couch again.

"I poured you a glass," he said, lifting the tumbler and swirling the amber liquid before taking a sip. "Unless you'd rather have tea, which I also made." He tipped his head, drawing my attention to the three drink options he had sitting on the table: the booze, a cup of tea, and a glass of water.

"Thank you." I carefully sat beside him, tucking my legs under me before reaching for the alcohol. I took a big drink and tried not to choke. "This is Vale's," I told him tightly as I fought not to gag at the taste. "I think it's gone bad." I sniffed it and took another cautious sip before chasing it with some water.

I felt the vibration of his chuckle through the couch. "This is how it's supposed to taste. It's not my top choice, but considering the swill I drank while I was in attendance here, it's not so bad." His eyes were warm as they roamed my face, and when he took in the position of my body, he tilted his head with his next question. "How are you feeling about everything?"

I shrugged, reaching for the liquid courage again, tossed back the remaining inch, and faced him. "I don't doubt you or our magic, but I'm overwhelmed at the instantaneous reveal and maybe slightly hysterical."

Khade's brows rose as he listened to me spiral. Clearing his throat, he sat his drink on the table before turning to face me. "Why?"

Pursing my lips, I looked down and picked at my nails. "Because. You're ... you."

I'd barely gotten the words out when he brushed a loose strand of hair behind my ear, his touch lingering on my cheek. "And you're the heir to the entire kingdom, Lyra. There isn't a power imbalance here."

I winced. Wasn't that similar to what Axel had said to me?

"That's not how I meant it," I whispered.

"I want to understand, but first, explain your reaction just then." His voice hardened, but I didn't get the feeling his mood change was directed at me. He was on the defense, not demanding something from me in anger.

"Can we skip the rejected mate details tonight?" That was the wrong thing to say and too much information.

The temperature in the room dropped; his eyes darkened, his jaw clenched, and suddenly, I was right next to him with my legs across his lap, his hands wrapped around my face, and his forehead pressed to mine.

There was a deep rattle, almost like a growl, coming from him as he breathed. "For now, yes. But I need to know soon, so I never accidentally say something to you that will cause you pain again." His tone and words were measured as he spoke, but I didn't think he was fighting his animal form or holding back a shift. Instead, he commanded a careful balance with the powerful beast within while holding me gently, as though I were fragile, but firm enough not to slip through his fingers and break.

I tried to nod but my head was immobile, and I tried to smile, but my face and cheeks were stuck between his palms, so I quietly agreed with words instead.

When he kissed me, it was one of reassurance. There was nothing but support and tenderness in the way he was comforting me, and the sweetness of it had me softening into him with his affection.

When he withdrew, his thumb swiped over my lower lip, leaving a tingling sensation in its path. Whether it was because of the contrast between his body heat and the chill in the room, or simply his touch, I wasn't sure. Either way, it felt nice and made me giddy inside.

After he released my face, his hands drifted up and down my arms, chasing away the shiver that had coursed through me. When his hands reached my legs, he tenderly massaged the lingering cool tension away until my muscles gradually eased in the warmth of his touch.

"Tell me why this is bothering you." His voice regained its steady cadence, and his features relaxed into a calm expression as he patiently awaited my response.

I sighed, then hid my face in my hands and dropped my head to rest against my knees with a huff. "It's embarrassing."

One of his hands wrapped around my ankle as the other sifted through my hair, trailing down my back. As awkward as I was acting, I was more than comfortable with his touch, as if his caress was casting away my unease like a soothing balm to my jumbled emotions.

I could feel the movement when he nodded, then after a moment, he sighed. "I'll tell you why I'm embarrassed, then. I'm ashamed I didn't conduct myself more professionally and keep my private life outside of the castle while I've been employed there. It's my job to consider all possible outcomes and respond and react accordingly. I failed to do that, and now, after meeting you today, I'm troubled by what you might have heard about me being whispered in the halls of your home."

I peeked at him over my arm as he spoke, and his discontent was clearly sketched on his face. But I didn't want him to feel that way. "Khade..."

"Is this something that has been bothering you as much as it has been bothering me?" His brows pinched when he asked.

"No." I took his hand in mine. "At least, not in the way I think you're implying. You had a life before me, just as I had one before you."

"You grew up hearing stories about mine."

"That doesn't bother me; your prior interactions don't bother me."

"Then what is it if not that?"

"Living up to you." My shoulders slumped as I took the opening and word-vomited all my insecurities out to him. "You're miles ahead of me in experience, your magic, and career, while I've never worked a day in my life. I've been sequestered inside a castle, hidden from the world. Even without the binding of the geas, I struggle to hold my shifted form. I don't even know if I'll be good at my job. I'm terrifyingly inexperienced, and I fear I'll drag you down."

"Lyra, from the day you were born, you've been preparing for a role understood only by your mother and grandmothers. It wasn't a choice you made or were given, yet you've devoted years to training for it. You've already achieved so much in readiness for a position you'll not hold for decades. While you may have lived a pampered life"—he smirked, and I returned the smile— "that existence came at a price. Being secluded from the freedoms others take for granted is not a small sacrifice. Give yourself some credit. You haven't been idle, and you're not a drain on society. You've accomplished more than most in this kingdom, and your journey is just beginning. If anyone should feel like a burden, it's me in regard to you."

"You're flattering me now."

"I'm not." He said with a straight face. "I will always be honest with you."

"I want that for all of us."

"Then you'll have it." He lifted my hand and kissed my knuckles. "Does the age difference bother you? Twelve years can seem like a lot right now."

I smirked at him and shook my head. "No. That doesn't bother me either."

"Good. And the sex and stories you've heard..."

My face flamed. I didn't even have time to blush. I instantly felt flush.

Khade ran a finger across my cheek as his eyes darkened. "I want you to always wear your emotions so plainly for me, but we'll need to work on this before you make public appearances."

"As long as I'm not asked about sex, I think I'll be fine."

"If anyone who shouldn't asks you about sex, it will be the last thing they do," he told me seriously, and after spending the last several hours with him and learning that he's sent people to the badlands on my behalf, I believed him.

"I'm not ... bothered about anything, Khade. Truly."

"Then allow me to say my peace, and we'll move past it." He kissed my cheek. "My past doesn't affect my present with you, just as yours doesn't with me. But I assure you, nothing we do together will be like anything from my history—not like you've heard. What we will share will be new. There are parts of me and my desires that I've saved for you. I've had time to hone my skills, and I promise—the things I will do to you, no one has ever experienced with me before." His voice was as deep as my breathing now.

My stomach was tight, and the hand he had rested on my leg felt hotter and heavier. The need to clench something had me holding back a whimper.

"More than that, Lyra, my goal is to have everything with you. I aim to know your mind, explore your hopes and dreams, and learn all your desires. I want to understand your emotions so I can always be attuned to your feelings. My wish is to make you my partner in life, and to build a family together. I want it all, Lyra. Everything."

"I want that too. More than anything." I wrapped my hands around his face and leaned in to kiss him. "And I want you to teach me..."

He closed the distance and kissed me hard; then, we made out on the couch like a couple of teenagers in a college dorm.

Chapter Five

Khade

I should put her to bed.

The thought swirled around my head like the amber liquid in my glass. Instead of acting on it, I sipped the whiskey and continued to stare at my little mate.

My mate.

Her breathing was even as she slept. One hand still curled under her cheek where she'd rested her head to talk to me. Every so often, her lashes would flutter as she dreamed. She looked perfectly at ease with her legs resting over my lap. She let out a contented sigh when I ran my thumb down the arch of her foot, and when I broke contact, a small pucker formed between her brows.

She liked me touching her, even in her sleep.

I liked that very much.

I was surprised the buttons on my shirt didn't pop off from my chest swelling.

I was surprised I didn't ruin my slacks earlier from ignoring my painfully hard cock.

Not claiming her took effort I wasn't accustomed to exerting. I had always found it easy to maintain my patience and control, but this time, it demanded conscious restraint.

I'd never wanted to fuck anyone as much as I wanted to claim my mate. Such a receptive little thing, too. Her sweet pussy perfumed the dorm with her arousal. Her need made her pliable and shivering under my touch. I couldn't wait to explore all the ways to make her quiver for me.

The reveal had happened so quickly though. I didn't just want her to know me—I required it.

My reputation preceded me, and I was certain, even without her admission, that growing up in that castle, she'd heard plenty. We all engaged in the basic desire for sex; I just happened to be very liberal with my indulgence. Had I realized my mate would hear those stories, I would have been more discreet. I would have never let a whisper enter the halls of court, that's for damn sure.

Being someone's fated mate didn't erase all doubt, and I needed her to know my intentions were pure. I wanted her to understand that she wasn't, and never would be, just another female I passed time with. Among all the things I had ever wanted and achieved in my life, she had remained elusive. But now that I finally had her, I was determined to do everything in my power to ensure she knew just how important she was to me.

Even if that meant waiting to complete the bond. I wasn't only interested in her physically; it was important to me that she was emotionally and mentally well cared for, especially after everything she'd already endured at the hands of that noble prick.

We'd spent the last couple of hours together, talking and getting to know each other. Our conversation went beyond surface level, given that I'd known and worked for her family for years and my public figure status. I could safely say we were no longer strangers fated to spend our lives together.

There was a sweet innocence about her I hadn't expected to find so endearing. A softness to her that was so different from my rigidity. My initial assumptions about her had stemmed from knowing her bold and boisterous family and the self-assuredness of the Queen.

There was a purity about Lyra that was different than I'd expected, whether it was due to her sequestered life or her inherent nature. I had yet to determine, but I was utterly smitten with my little mate. The way her smile lighted up her eyes when she spoke of her family and friends, and the charming way she viewed the world as if embracing it. Which was a far cry from the calculated way I viewed it required by my position. There was strength in her compassion that should not be mistaken for naivety or weakness.

While we were discussing her classwork, her eyes grew heavy until she gradually drifted off to sleep, which filled me with a sense of pride in her comfort with me.

I could spend all night watching her sleep, but a stronger need to protect her conflicted with my desire to be near her, and learn more about her and the threats being made against her. So, I finally relented, shifting us around just enough to move without waking her.

Lifting her into my arms felt so natural, as if my muscles had memory and missed holding her in my arms even though I never had. An irrational instinct to curse the stars for putting us in our positions had me tightening my hold around her. If she had been anyone else, I wouldn't be faced with the task of fighting off endless enemies and could instead spend my days in carefree bliss with her. The NNC was just the latest threat in a lifetime of adversaries that she would face, and by proxy, us—her Knights.

But then she wouldn't be precisely who she was, and the thought of not having her exactly as she was stung me deeply enough to thank fate and be grateful instead.

As she rested her head against my shoulder, she stirred enough to bury her nose in the crook of my neck and wrap her arm around me.

"Sorry, I fell asleep," she mumbled dreamily—something I was sure she wouldn't even remember saying tomorrow.

"Never apologize for sleeping in my arms, beauty," I whispered against her cheek, nuzzling her as I walked the short distance down the hallway, taking in the space as a plan formed in my mind.

In her room, after I pulled apart the sheets, I reluctantly laid her down in the middle of a bed big enough for five. I wanted to climb in beside her, but it was too soon for that. Watching her burrow herself in the bed she shared with Vale only bothered me because it was vacant of my scent.

That would not be the case for long.

I watched her for another moment until her breathing evened out before I left her to rest. Making my way back out into the small kitchen of her dorm, I made myself at home, acquainting myself with the space before getting to work. Most of the information I'd requested earlier tonight, I'd already been privy to. All the criminal cases involving her, I prosecuted myself—traitors who threatened the crown and the safety of my mate before I knew she was mine. I felt even more relieved and justified in the relentless pursuit I enacted against them. That they would never be a threat to her again and were banished from the kingdoms to a place worse than death made me gloat in triumph.

There weren't many, but even one was too much, and a pattern became apparent as I examined them with a fresh perspective. Their frequency had notably risen over the past few years, coinciding with the emergence of rumors about the New Night Coalition and their aim to overturn the current rule. A trend I might have missed had I not been fated mates with the next queen—something easily overlooked without connecting it to the NNC and their rhetoric.

"What are you doing?" Vale's deep voice broke through the near silence of the room as he closed the door behind him with barely a sound.

"Research," I told him as I shuffled through another stack of papers.

"Is she in bed?" he asked, slipping his shoes off before coming to stand next to the table that I'd made my temporary desk.

"She is." I turned my laptop around to face him. "Go through this and tell me what's missing from this report."

"Sure, Khade, I'll help you. No, I wasn't looking forward to crashing next to my mate after a long day. Yes, I'd much rather do this right now instead of tomorrow after a full night's sleep. Thanks for asking." The dragon shifter's voice was bored sarcasm, but he bent over the table to do as I'd asked, scrolling through the file labeled "Axel Stonebrook".

As he did so, I sifted through the other files in front of me, other names that held suspicion and sat at the top of a list of suspected traitors. One of which was Azael, Axel's father. He'd been making himself a problem for years. When his son rejected the unknown female, my disdain for their family had intensified. Now that I knew who that female was, Azael's antagonism was even more questionable than before.

"You know this report is going to be thorough," Vale remarked as he scanned the document.

"Yes, but I also know more has happened since the first logs were made. You're his best friend. You should have been reviewing it anyway to ensure its accuracy and updating it frequently."

"Ex-best friend, and I've given statements and revised several reports already."

"That's not good enough."

Vale snapped his head up, glaring at me. "Excuse me?"

"I understand the family wanted you two to enjoy your time here. In a perfect world, that would be ideal. Unfortunately, tyranny doesn't wait for graduation dates, and as one of Lyra's mates, I will not keep information from her, you, or any others who join us. It's not my place to know more than you or my future queen. So, unfortunately, your limited knowledge and minimal involvement have ended. Giving reports when something happens or when they ask for updated information isn't enough. This is equally as personal as it is professional, and you should consider your time spent with Axel as undercover work for the crown. That includes constant updates of everything he shares with you at every turn."

Vale's brow raised, and then his face relaxed as he suppressed the vitriol he was probably ready to spew. Instead, he smirked at me. "Good. I wanted to be more involved from the beginning, but as a student trying to decide which direction to take in life, it's been a challenging demand to make for myself."

"I don't have that problem," I was relieved that Vale was on board and willing to follow my lead. "Leave it to me for now. We're a team, and as Lyra's mate, your opinions, ideas, and support are important."

Vale nodded and dropped into the chair beside me. "Anything you want or need to keep her safe, I'll give you."

"Then tell me what I don't already know about Axel."

"That's a long list." He sighed, and the wood creaked under his weight as he settled in.

"Then stick to the important details where it concerns Lyra," I told him before giving him time to sort through his thoughts.

While I waited, I made a mental note and added reinforced furniture to the list of improvements I would make here. The bed was custom, but the rest of the items were standard issue for a dorm. Keeping up appearances was one thing, but constantly replacing dining room chairs because of a dragon shifter's use was a minor inconvenience I didn't want to deal with when it was an easy upgrade with a simple explanation.

"Other than what I'm adding to this report, there's not much..."

I sat back and looked up at him. "Try again."

He rolled his eyes and huffed out at me. "That's going to get fucking old."

"Don't lie to me, then, and it won't be a problem." I raised my brows, waiting for his response.

"What do you want to know? What we talked about tonight?"

"Yes. But first, what else have you been keeping from her other than his unwelcome visits?"

He shook his head. "Nothing."

I squinted at him.

"Nothing that I can prove." He crossed his arms over his chest. "When we were kids, he could make objects disappear."

"His divination is affliction. Are you saying he has magic in invisibility?"

"I'm saying he could hide things from me as a kid. Could he have developed the ability? Yes. But should he have? No."

"Because that's a high-powered talent, and he rejected the mate bond." I nodded.

"Or so he says, but yeah." Vale shrugged and shifted again in the creaky chair.

"I'm not ready to believe his victimhood or his forced coercion just yet. But let's say it's true, and he's made progress in invisibility magic. How is he using it concerning Lyra? And why hasn't this been brought up before?"

"I didn't tell her for the same reason I didn't mention he'd been here. I didn't want to worry her until I knew for sure. But I'm not keeping secrets or playing fast and loose with her safety. The Queen, Knight Lords, and the Dukes know of my suspicion. It was agreed that until there's proof, it shouldn't be mentioned to her. She's been through enough. Especially from him."

"How is he using it, Vale?"

He shrugged. "If he is, he's watching her, following her around."

"What is the family doing about it?"

"Looking into a detection spell." He sat forward and started tapping on the laptop again. "It's not so simple to detect because it's his divination magic, not just a spell someone is casting."

As my mind spun new possibilities, Vale was content to leave me to my thoughts and update Axel's files.

Stripping something inherent and coded into a fae's DNA wasn't the same as dispelling phrases of an incantation. A spell was a combination of words and intent, whereas divination magic was intricately woven into a person's identity—it was them, their mind and body, just as much as the shifted form. Each individual harnessed divination magic uniquely, so writing a spell to detect it would be quite a complex task. Especially if it was only speculation.

An hour later, Vale stretched with a grunt and turned the laptop back around to me, just as a message came through on my phone.

"Those are as updated as they're going to get for now. Unless you want me to steal his diary or write a novel about our childhood days."

I fired off a response to the sender before looking up at him. "If you think it will help."

His words were garbled as he yawned. "You're gonna need to chill out, man. Lyra's too sweet for this level of intensity." He gave the table a casual smack that made everything on it rattle.

"Lyra is my perfect match and counterpart in every way. Mind your own mate bond. I'll handle mine." I stood with him, then went to open the door as he shuffled down the hall to the bedroom. I took it as a good sign that he was unbothered by someone being here and trusting me to handle it.

"Of all the fucking people in the realms she could have mated, why'd it have to be you?" Shea shook his head and brushed past me. "If this is how it's going to be, you need to vet another portal caster."

"Not likely, Night Duke." I shoved the door, then caught the handle to keep it from slamming shut and waking my sleeping mate.

My mate.

I'd never tire of that.

Chapter Six

I woke warm and cozy, wrapped in Vale's arms with my face pressed against his chest.

My sunshine.

Smiling against his skin, I chuckled at the thought of calling him that. He really was like my personal sun; he'd come into my darkest night and brightened my day.

"What's funny, my mate?" As he hugged me tighter, he slid his knee between my thighs and lifted my leg to rest over him, allowing me to feel his morning wood.

Humming at the feel of him, I mumbled into his skin between kisses. "Nothing's funny," I told him as I reached between us, sliding my hand into his boxers to fist his cock. Kissing over his chest, I pumped him and found one of his nipples, flicking it with my tongue and pulling it between my lips.

He groaned and jerked in my hand. "Fuck, Lyra," he panted, cradling my head and rolling his hips into my working hand. "You have no idea how badly I want you, but—"

His words cut off with a groan as I circled the silky crown with my thumb and shifted around to grind my sex over his. I had every intention of pulling him free, moving my panties to the side, and sliding myself down onto him, but his next words stilled me.

"Khade is in the kitchen, and I think he made coffee." Vale cupped my face to look me in the eyes. "I am more than happy to continue, unless you'd rather wait until later." He smirked at me.

I was torn.

I really wanted to continue, especially after my make-out session with Khade and his promise to teach me. But Khade and I hadn't bonded yet. Was it rude to fuck my first mate while my other waited for me in the next room? I didn't know how to balance this yet, but I didn't want to hurt anyone. How did I divide my attention and prevent jealousy from creeping in? Could this be perceived as favoritism?

Khade had assured me and insisted we would get to know each other first, but I couldn't help but feel like I was choosing more with Vale right now. What if it was Vale on the other side of the door? The thought of causing him pain and making him feel left out made my heart feel heavy. Each of them deserved my attention, and the weight of being fair and considerate had me gnawing at my lips anxiously.

With a groan, I dropped my head onto Vale's chest, my mind suddenly overwhelmed with questions and no obvious answers.

"Do you want me to decide for you?" Vale's hot breath wove through the strands of my hair to heat my scalp as his heavy hands pawed and rubbed up and down my body.

It was easy to guess what he would choose, but I nodded anyway, to which he flipped me over, pulled off my pajama bottoms, and shoved his boxers down all in one go. Then he notched himself against me and pushed his fat cock into me slowly. My surprised squeal quickly turned into a moan as I spread myself wider for him.

"Learning to share is part of a growing mate bond." He moaned as he watched himself disappear into my body.

He took me hard and fast, and after I cried out his name with my release, he coated my belly with his. Then we showered together; he braced me against the wall and did it again.

An hour later, I emerged from my room and thanked the stars our bedroom was spelled for privacy because we weren't alone, and it wasn't just my winter mate awake and waiting in my dorm.

"Good morning." Khade looked me up and down with a twinkle in his eye as he handed me a cup of coffee, then bent and kissed my forehead, lingering there for a moment to breathe me in.

"Good morning." I smiled up at him, thankful for the time we'd spent together last night because I didn't feel so shell-shocked and shy with him anymore.

"All Hail the Queen, who finally rolled out of bed to join us," Puck grumbled from the table. "It's the weekend, you know. I should be sleeping in with my mate too, but noooo... You went and pulled a literal psycho into your mate bond, and now we don't get days off," he snarked before stuffing a white-powdered donut into his mouth, then went back to flipping through whatever pages he was looking at.

With each cranky word out of Puck's mouth, I felt my eyebrows try to disappear into my hairline.

"Your brother doesn't understand what the word 'literal' means, but he has a firm grasp on complaining." Khade put his hand on the small of my back and walked me to the table, where he pulled out a chair for me to sit.

Puck gave him a powdery smirk. "I stand by what I said."

"As do I." Khade's tone was anything but amused.

"If you stopped stalling and complaining, you would be done by now and back in bed with your mate," Tunder told Puck without looking up from his writing. "But between the bitching and moaning, and gorging on enough sugar to open a bakery, you're the reason you're still here. No one else."

Puck made a face and silently mocked him, which made me chuckle and him smirk at me. "Morning, Lala."

Rolling my eyes at him, I looked over the table. "What is all this?"

A buffet of food stretched down the center of the table, amidst plates, drinks, stacks of papers, folders, and open laptops, each facing one of them as they ate and worked.

"I told you, your mate is a psy—"

Tunder smacked Puck in the face with a folder. "We're filling in gaps in the reporting and acting as an extra line of protection at the moment. We've barely been here an hour. Puck's just whining like usual."

"Then why isn't Shea here? Hmm..." Puck yanked the folder out of Tunder's hand and dropped it onto a pile next to him. Then he turned to Tunder again, took a huge bite of his donut, and chewed it obnoxiously in his face.

"Shea did what I asked, quickly and efficiently, and then he left." Khade took a plate from the stack on the table and piled it with fresh fruit.

"And quietly." Tunder pushed Puck's head away. "You're disgusting. How old are you?" He wrinkled his nose and brushed his hand over the papers, then looked up at me when I failed to hide my amusement. "Don't encourage him. He's being extra, extra today, and that will only worsen if you egg him on."

I shrugged. Puck and his antics didn't bother me nearly as much as they bothered my brothers, which just added to the fun I got out of it. But since he was obviously annoyed, I resisted teasing him more. "What did Shea do when he was here?"

"He put in a private portal." Tunder tipped his head toward the hallway.

"Which I'm going to use now that I've finished," Cleon said, coming in from the balcony, followed by a strange man I'd never seen before.

"What—" My words cut off with a squeak as I whipped my head around and blocked my face. "Who is that?" I whispered, turning my body away from the unknown. My glamour was intact, but we were in my dorm with the Night Lords and the Queen's Council, which was sure to raise questions.

Khade's cool fingers wrapped around my wrists, guiding my hands away from my face to meet his gaze. "Your brother has been supervising Caldor while he's been under my thrall. He's an enchantment specialist. There's nothing to worry about," he assured me, his eyes fixed on mine. I nodded in response, and he handed me a cup, shifting his attention to Cleon and Caldor. "Is it done?"

"Yes," the man answered him in a numb, detached manner. His eyes were glossed over and unfocused, devoid of any emotion, and there was no inflection in his tone when he spoke. He stood ramrod straight, with his arms hanging loosely at his sides as he gazed blankly ahead. "I've cast the Sanctum Ward to your exact specifications, and as you know, I guarantee my work, Mr. Ranehall."

"I know you do." Khade moved and patted the guy on the shoulder. "Thank you, Caldor."

The man should have flinched or reacted in some way to Khade's touch or words, but he didn't. He just stood there like a talking statue. I'd read examples and heard plenty about Sensory Compulsion, but I'd never seen it in action before. Khade didn't appear as though he was exerting any effort using his Divination Magic on the enchantment specialist either. His focus wasn't split, and he didn't appear to be concentrating. He was simply overriding the man's senses. It was a little terrifying. Or it would be if it were anyone else doing it and not the trusted Night Court councilor.

"He re-spelled the building and fortified the entire floor and apartment," Cleon added, but since he was looking at me, I knew it was only for my benefit. Then, refocusing on Khade, he continued, "The whole level was going to stay vacant while she was here anyway, but with what Caldor wove into the protection spell, I doubt anyone would voluntarily move in or stay if they did. The disconcerting charm will see to that."

"Good." Khade nodded in approval. "That's exactly what I requested."

Puck leaned forward to get my attention. "See? Psycho." He raised his brows and widened his eyes, then let out an "oof" when Tunder elbowed him. "Ow, ass."

"Just please stop talking." Tunder shook his head at him.

"You stop talking," Puck mocked.

"I'll speak to the Knight Lords about your other request and get back to you as soon as I hear anything," Cleon told Khade.

Khade gave him a nod before turning to me. "I'll return in a few minutes," he said, taking Caldor's elbow to lead him through the small dorm and down the hall.

"You have your hands full." Cleon patted the top of my head as he walked by. "I'd love to stay and chat, but I was pulled from bed to be here and I want to get back to it. Bye, Lala," he hollered over his shoulder before also disappearing down the hallway and through a door that had been a closet yesterday.

"What is going on?" I looked to Vale, who had just finished piling food on a plate.

"Upgrades. But I'll let Khade explain himself." He put his arm around the back of my chair and bit into a chocolate donut, taking half in one go.

"You know those billionaire mafia romance novels the Day Princess always gave you to read?" Puck waggled his brows up and down at me.

"You mean the ones you two would read together and then pretend they were mine when Mom caught you with them?"

"Not the point." He shook his head and stabbed a chunk of pineapple with his fork. "The point is, your new mate is acting the part. Which would be hot as fuck if it wasn't him—because of two reasons: he's a dick and your mate, which is super gross. This whole bossy boss thing he does would be so much better if it was one of my mates instead."

"He's not a crime lord!" I threw a blueberry at him. "And he's not a dick."

"Again, not the point, and yes, he is."

"You still read them, don't you?" Vale smirked at him.

"It's not a sin."

"Does Roko know?"

Puck rolled his eyes. "Duh, we read them together in bed. Then we act out the—"

"Stop." Vale lifted his hand. "I don't want to know. Forget I asked."

They argued while Tunder ignored the table to work and I ate my breakfast. Other than the stacks of folders and papers and laptops scattered around the dorm, I couldn't see anything different that had been changed or upgraded in the space. I didn't feel any new magic either.

Curiosity got the best of me, and when I stepped through the sliding door onto the balcony, I felt the first changes of the new magic that had been placed around the space. It didn't look any different, but there was an added weight that hadn't been there before.

"If someone has bad intentions, the additional barrier will ward them away and an alert will be triggered." Khade's voice surprised me, and I turned to find him right behind me. "I didn't mean to startle you. We'll work on that too." He lifted my hand and kissed my knuckles. "I hope you don't mind, but I took the liberty of speaking with your parents and the High Priestess about modifying your geas at will, so you can practice your shifting at a secure location."

He wasn't talking down to me, which I was grateful for. But I was still embarrassed because if my geas hadn't been in control, I would have definitely puffed into smoke just then.

He stared at me before leaning down to put his face in front of mine. "You have nothing to be embarrassed about, Lyra. It took me years to master my shifted form fully, and I had the freedom to learn and grow without constraints, unlike you. You will never receive judgment from me. Is that clear?"

I couldn't speak, so I nodded instead. Our conversation last night had eased a lot of my insecurity with him, but hearing about something and seeing it nearly happen were two different things. I didn't expect him to laugh at me, but I was still grateful that he didn't.

"Good." The single word sounded like a command, and my nipples pinched at his tone as my breath hitched.

Khade's pupils blew wide as he closed the space, kissing me hard and wrapping his hands around my face to hold me in place. It was quick but thorough, and though I'd had multiple orgasms this morning with Vale, I felt the yearning to experience another. This time with Khade.

"Did I overstep?" He wiped my swollen lips as he stood to his full height.

"No," I assured him. "I appreciate the additional training time."

"If I ever do, don't hesitate to put me in my place." He smirked, which made me blush. The thought of bossing him around had an appeal that wasn't about either of our positions.

His pupils slitted as a low rattle emanated from his chest, but rather than commenting, he carried on. "Let me further explain what I've done here overnight and this morning. I'll show you the modifications that have been made to the dorm, then we'll talk about the geas and the additional changes I've requested."

"Further changes? Is there something wrong with it?" My brows lifted as the blood drained from my cheeks. If anything was wrong with the concealment...

"The geas is still intact and working as expected. I will explain everything, but first"—he took my hand and walked me to the railing, where he pointed out around us—"the Sanctum Ward I had placed today extends further around the building, but more specifically, deeper into the forest. The windows of your dorm that face the forest were a security risk, so the new spell is as much for safety as it is for distraction." He led me to the stairs as if to walk down together where anyone could be.

"Someone will see us." I stopped.

Khade turned and gave me a placating smile. "Trust me."

And I did, so I followed him down the stairs and across the small lawn until we were under the cover of trees in the forest.

When we stopped and turned to face the building again, I was amazed at how full the vining geum flowers were. They practically covered the entire backside of the dorm, climbing from a large bush and reaching over the roof where they ran along the edge to dangle down. They were beautiful.

"They're so pretty." I marveled at my favorite flower.

Khade squinted at the flowers but didn't comment. He had secondary earth magic, but his Imperium Talent was for water; I guessed he, like Vale, wasn't as excited about plants as I was. Instead, he detailed the extra protections he'd had put into place. "The Sanctum Ward holds a mirage spell. When someone is in the dorm, shadowy silhouettes will appear in the windows and lights will turn on and off as you use them, but no one will see into the space any longer."

"I didn't realize that was something to be concerned about." I wrinkled my brow at the thought of being watched.

"I was surprised it wasn't addressed, but I doubt your family expected it to be a concern." Before I could fully consider his words, he moved to stand in front of me, then turned a ring on his finger, and became a spitting image of Vale.

"Oh!" I covered my mouth in shock. "That's … bizarre."

He chuckled, which made the whole thing extra disorienting because it was his voice coming from Vale's face. "It is. I don't intend to use it often."

He pulled out his phone and sent a message, then pointed my attention to the balcony again. Vale stepped out of the dorm and looked around. When he found us, he tipped his head back in silent laughter, and I felt a smile take over my face at his obvious enjoyment.

Behind him, a shadow appeared in the door and moved around, pacing back and forth while waving hands in the air. But no matter what they did, I couldn't see who it was or hear what Vale was saying to them or us as he pointed in our direction. I assumed the person in the dorm was Puck, based on the movements, just as I was certain they were both having a good laugh at Khade for wearing Vale's face.

"Someone who isn't a threat will be able to pass the barrier," Khade explained. "But no one will see into the dorm anymore. All the windows and doors are opaque and spelled, and from this distance, sound is distorted." Then he stepped behind me, placed his hands on my waist, and guided us back until we were on the other side of the enchantment. Vale disappeared in an instant, but the shadowy figure in the window remained.

"Anyone with ill intent will only see this view. Their proximity becomes unbearable for those who are potential threats. You can't feel it because you are not a threat to yourself, but for someone who is, every instinct they have will require they leave the area as immediately as possible," he told me. "Regardless, anyone who approaches this closely from this direction will trigger a safety measure, and an alert will be sent to each of us, your family included."

"What happens if someone goes beyond the barrier? Good or bad?" I was more than curious now. I didn't believe I was in any danger here. My family would have already made sure of that. But what he'd done had my interest piqued, and the insatiable part of my brain that thirsted for knowledge wanted to know everything.

"Those who pose no threat, nothing will happen but an alert to us."

"And those who do?"

"For someone dangerous—'if' is a very big word—but if they manage it, there is a defensive layer woven into the spell."

"What kind?" I turned in his arms to look up at him. "Will it hurt them? What about those already inside the barrier when the spell is triggered?"

He considered my question before answering, "Nothing permanent."

"What does that mean?" I wasn't too keen on being responsible for injuring anyone, even if by proxy.

His demeanor relaxed with understanding at my expression, which must have shown my discomfort at the idea. "A high-pitched tone will render them and anyone else in the boundary unconscious, aside from you, Vale, your family, and myself."

"Has it been tested? How do we know it will work?"

He smirked. "It's been tested by the guard and has been used in the past. It's not an original design, and I can't take all the credit for thinking of it. I called in a favor from a guardsman, who cased the exterior for vulnerabilities."

"Won't that raise questions?" Every time he told me something about his additions to my security detail, it brought up more concerns of exposure.

He bent and kissed me, which was weird. His lips felt like his, even though his face looked like Vale. "I like how your mind works." He smirked. "It won't raise questions. I may have pissed off my contact with my favor. To keep him from growing suspicious, I had him scout all the facility quarters, dorms, and mated buildings for security weak points. He's currently evaluating all ancillary facilities for vulnerabilities as well. It's not entirely a ruse, considering everything going on and that you could be in any of these buildings at any time, but admittedly, it is a stretch. When he's finished, he'll report his findings as official, working under orders, and I'll submit mine as well."

"But won't he still question why you're having him do it? It's a bit random, isn't it?"

"No. I have a cousin who teaches here and stays on-site while class is in session. He may be curious about what I know that he doesn't and why I've asked for the report, but he won't question it in any way that would arouse suspicions or prompt anyone else." He kissed my head and then put his hand on the small of my back as we walked past the barrier again and inside the dorm.

"You know, Khade, if you wore that glamour and then if you and Vale fucked Lyra at the same time, it would be like double dirty twin delight," Puck said to us as casually as if he'd said it was going to rain.

"Puck!"

"What?" He looked up at me from his phone. "I'm just saying." He shrugged.

"And I'm out." Tunder came over and kissed me on the cheek. "See you at family dinner, Lala. You two, try not to kill him." He looked at each of my mates and then at Puck before disappearing down the hall and into the closet.

"My life wouldn't be in danger if I could just—"

"Leave." Khade reached across the table and snapped the laptop closed.

"Really?"

"Now."

Puck dropped his feet from the table and gave us a peace sign over his shoulder as he left. "Later, losers."

"You'll get used to him." Vale stretched his arms out with a groan, making his already wide chest flex wider. "But if you ever want to role-play..." He waggled his brows.

"No."

Khade took my hand again, ignoring Vale and his comment, and walked me down the hall. "Let me explain the closet."

Chapter Seven

"This portal opens into the secret alcove outside of Araphel's gates," Khade explained before we walked into the closet that used to hold my jackets and extra shoes but now held a shimmering travel gate.

In an instant, I was standing inside the windowless room that I'd become accustomed to since my first day at the school. Now, however, instead of just the one travel portal that led to the castle, there were two additional ones next to it.

"Shea was up most of the night putting these in." Khade stood in front of the new portals, calm and confident, while I nearly tripped with surprise.

I marveled at my brother's skill. Portal casting was strong magic that required a focused mind and precision akin to a surgeon's hand. If even a single degree in the coordinates was wrong, you could be transported from where you wanted to go safely to instead casting you off in the middle of nowhere. Sometimes never to be seen again.

"That's a lot of work."

"Yes, it was," he stated indifferently to the heavy feat my eldest brother had performed.

Vale wrapped his arm around my shoulder and pulled me against him. "I'm sure what Khade means is that he's grateful for what your brother did for us, and he recognizes the effort it took for him to do it in just a few hours."

"Of course." Khade's brows drew down but then lifted with realization when he looked at me. "His work is appreciated, and I told him as much when he finished." He took my hand again, then looked up at Vale. "But it's also his job, and he was heavily compensated for it."

"I'm beginning to understand why Lyra's brothers have an admire and revolt relationship with you." Vale shook his head.

Khade didn't take what my brother had done lightly, or he wouldn't have asked Shea to do the work. I knew that from his reputation alone. Khade upheld a high standard in his work, one that he expected others to meet as well. My winter mate just didn't seem the type to offer kudos in excess while Vale, on the other hand, was generous with his.

Khade was unfazed by the snark and held Vale's eyes with a steady gaze before focusing on the portals again. "This one will bring you to an adjacent room at my private office at the Night Court. The room has been spelled for concealment, and I'll be alerted upon your arrival."

"Isn't this portal redundant? There's already one at the castle." Vale stepped up to Khade's office portal and stuck his hand through.

"The castle is a big place, and I value my time. This will make my commute that much faster and will bring Lyra directly to me whenever she wants."

It was a very logical explanation, and he was correct. The portal that led into my family's private quarters was on the clear opposite side of where staff offices were located. It was at least a ten-minute walk, and that was only if you weren't stopped along the way.

"Where does this one go?" I asked about the third portal.

"That leads to our private home in the middle of the Norshire Wood Mountains in the Winter Realm."

I was sure I'd misheard him. "Our what?"

Khade gave a warm chuckle. "I'll show you later." He took my hand and pulled me along with him, stepping through the portal I was familiar with, which took us into the receiving room of my childhood home.

"What are we doing here?" I asked him while we waited for Vale to follow.

Khade ran his hand down the side of my face. "We have a matter to discuss with your family. They're expecting us. It's nothing to worry about," he said, but that had the exact opposite effect.

"Now I feel like I should be worried about not being worried rather than just being worried."

His eyebrows lifted as I rambled, and that little smirk played at the corners of his lips as he bent down and opened his mouth as if to respond, but Vale interrupted as he bounded through the portal.

"You have a nice office. It's as big as I expected, and the dark wood, sturdy furniture, and massive fireplace are on brand." Vale sauntered up next to us, twirling something in his fingers. "And you have great pens."

Khade didn't move his hand from where he held my chin, or change the way he was leaning in toward me, but he looked up at Vale as he kissed my forehead. "What's mine is yours," he told him dryly.

Vale rested his arm around my shoulder and dropped his head to my ear. "See, he knows how to share."

Khade's eyes darkened, my face heated, and Vale's lips were a smile against my temple.

Khade cleared his throat as he took my hand and led us to the dining room, where my parents were waiting.

"Hi, my darling." Papa pulled me into a hug while my other parents greeted my two mates. "You've had a busy couple of days. How are you?" he whispered in my ear.

I snuggled up into his chest, resting my cheek on his shirt. "Really good, Papa." I sighed into his comforting embrace, keeping my arms around his as I greeted my other dads until my mother pulled us apart.

"My turn." She smiled with her arms out for me. "You look happy, Lala." Her warm breath wove through the strands of my hair as she whispered to me.

"I am." I let her wrap me up and hold me like a child for a few moments. Adulting was hard, and I'd only just begun. But I was happy.

"Chef made your favorite." Father kissed my head before going over and pulling out the chair for my mother to sit—his not-so-subtle way to get things moving.

Khade did the same, pulling my chair out for me. Vale went around us to my other side as he stared down at my winter mate. "I usually sit her on my lap, but sure, the cold hard chair works too," he goaded, making me blush again.

"I'm beginning to understand your bromance with Puck," Khade snarked, volleying back Vale's earlier remark, which surprised me enough that I blurted out a laugh.

Vale was clearly relaxed with the addition of Khade into our bond, and I was giddy seeing Khade thaw to Vale's charm so quickly too. I didn't want to admit even to myself how worried I was about the relationships between my mates. I didn't want there to be mistrust and reluctance between them because of the scars left behind from the rejection, but it wasn't unreasonable to assume that each of my mates would exercise caution with the others because of it. I was glad that I was wrong, at least where these two were concerned. We were already going to face more pressures than other mated groups, and with the threat of the NNC on top of everything else, it was nice to see them settling with each other so rapidly.

"I see you two are adjusting nicely," Pai commented behind the coffee cup he was lifting to his lips. "That's good. It took Noel a year to like me."

"The jury's still out." Father's voice was laced with humor, and he winked at me when I smiled up at him. I didn't need his reassurance that he was teasing, but I was glad to have it.

My parents didn't have conflict in their mate group—none that we children were aware of, anyway. Their relationship was something I'd admired growing up, and it formed the basis of my expectations for what a mate bond should be like, which was why I was so shattered when it didn't happen the same way for me.

It was another reason I was so happy right now because I could safely say that was no longer the case. I was finally living my dream.

"Please, everyone, help yourselves to some food. We can chat while enjoying our brunch," my mother instructed us.

"I didn't know we were coming for brunch, and I ate this morning," I said, skipping the food and going for the coffee. Honestly, I was more interested in getting to the topic of why we were here. I knew something more than breakfast with my parents was on the menu today.

"You picked at some fruit and drank coffee," Khade said, pouring me a glass of orange juice and eyeing the caffeine I was flavoring with cream.

"That wasn't eating, my mate." Vale tsked, agreeing with Khade as he served me a helping of honeymoon eggs with extra hollandaise.

It smelled delicious, so I didn't bother to argue further when he sat it in front of me. It was my favorite, and my mouth swam with anticipation as I dug in, giving him a hasty, "Thank you."

"Oh, we have a happy dance." Baba chuckled.

I didn't even care they were laughing at me. I hadn't had chef's eggs benedict in months, and I might as well enjoy them until they all decided to get to the point. "It's yummy." I shrugged and shoveled another bite into my mouth.

After Vale and Khade dished themselves, my parents made small talk with them while we ate. It was so comfortable and casual I quickly forgot I was supposed to be worried about why we were here, until we were done eating and the mood in the room shifted in an instant.

"So, let's get into it." Father sipped from his mug before setting it down to focus on Khade. "We spoke with the High Priestess about the added enchantment you want spelled into the geas. She's looking into it as we speak. Now that it's being taken to this degree, please inform your mate."

My heart raced in my chest. Father didn't seem angry as he addressed and instructed Khade, but I felt like I should be. Everyone in the room knew something important, something significant enough to warrant changing the spell that concealed my identity.

"Of course." Khade gave him a quick nod, then turned to face my summer mate pointedly. "Vale?"

Every eye in the room, including mine, fell on him. He looked like he wanted to crawl into a hole.

"Thanks." He glared at Khade before turning his eyes down to me. "You know I would never do anything that would put you in danger." His voice was stern.

"I know."

"I would never keep anything from you unless I felt it was in your best interest." I prickled at that. Vale took my hand and pleaded with his eyes, a plea for understanding laced through our bond as he continued. "I didn't say anything because I don't have proof, and I didn't want to worry you unnecessarily."

"Okay..."

"He was also under orders not to," my mother spoke up in his defense.

Vale nodded enthusiastically at her statement. "And that."

I deflated a little as my ire abated. If he were under an order from my mother, I couldn't exactly be mad about it. She was the Queen, after all.

"Please, just tell me."

He sighed and gave me a little smile. "There is a possibility that Axel has progressed in invisibility magic and he's behind the odd sensations you're getting."

I slumped in my chair and listened as he went on to explain how growing up with Axel, he used to play tricks on him with his ability by hiding things.

"How long have you suspected he was following me?" I asked, unsure whether I should be upset about not being informed. He'd put himself in this predicament by approaching my family before me, which meant he couldn't have told me without permission. Though I wished he had come to me first, I understood his choice. It was all very confusing.

"A couple of weeks. I'm sorry, Lyra. I should have told you," he said, looking like someone had kicked his puppy. He was defeated. "I didn't want you to worry, and I didn't want to believe it to be true..."

"But?"

"You had the sensation of being watched on our way home last night, and then immediately after Axel showed up on the balcony."

Taking his random appearance into account, it seemed likely that he was the reason behind the feeling of being followed. He could have easily beaten us to the dorm and waited outside on the balcony until we arrived. If I didn't want someone to know I was following them but still wanted to be seen, it's what I would have done.

"How many times have you felt like you were being watched before last night?" Papa asked.

"Just a handful of times." I shrugged, recounting the instances to them.

"And you never felt like you were in danger?" Pai questioned.

"No, not in danger necessarily." I shook my head. "Each time it's happened has been a little different, though. Sometimes, it creeps me out; other times, it just feels like there are eyes on me. I get this tingling sensation, but nothing alarming. What does this have to do with the geas?"

My parents looked at Khade when I asked, but he was looking at me when he explained, "As you know, it's difficult to counteract Divination Magic with a spell."

I nodded. Our magic was part of who we were, like the color of our eyes or the points of our ears. Outside influences could affect it for a time, but the only true balance to one was having the contrary to another. In the elemental cycle, fire was doused with water, water was absorbed by earth, earth was eroded by air, and air suffocated fire. It was the same for our Divination Magic.

Papa's Affliction was Ergokinetic Armor. He could create energy armor and shield himself or others in energetic plating that acted as a barrier against physical attacks. Baba's counter to that was his Sensory Divination of Energy Transference. Baba could redirect energy from an individual or an object to another. So Papa could armor himself and others, and while Baba couldn't necessarily pull the energy from Papa's own armor directly, Baba could dispel it if it was cast on another by redirecting the energy to a nearby object or dissipating it into the environment.

In everything, there was a complementary opposite.

"With my abilities now linked through you and into the bond," Khade continued, "the High Priestess believes she can tap into my Truthsayer ability and my Sensory Compulsion or the Mental Petrification that's developing. We believe we can manipulate the geas, which will allow us to see him."

I was at a loss for words. That was potent magic. The geas was already a powerful spell that was more than just hiding my appearance; it dampened my abilities and had its own safeguards and protections woven into the incantation. But to tap into Khade's skill and bolster it into an already dynamic power was nothing I'd ever heard of before.

Not to mention that he'd just casually admitted to developing a Mental Petrification ability. This magic granted the wielder complete control over someone's mind, rendering them mentally paralyzed by freezing their thoughts, emotions, and processes—sometimes permanently. His Sensory Compulsion already gave him access to compel or manipulate the senses of others, allowing him to heighten, diminish, or alter sight, hearing, touch, taste, and smell. Khade wasn't just respected and feared for his deadly shifter abilities and the lethal venom he held in that form; his unassailable prowess as a prosecutor cemented his reputation, even without his Truthsayer gift. His Sensory Compulsion was also well-known—both professionally and personally. It was how he'd controlled Caldor, the enchantment specialist, earlier this morning. The addition of Mental Petrification was staggering. The two abilities were similar, but it was rare for both to be held by a single individual.

I felt average next to him again, but my chest swelled with pride. Khade was mine, and I was a little smug about it. My face must have shown the shock and awe I was feeling because he gave me his barely there smirk.

"I was surprised as well. I'm not fully able to access the petrification, but I know what it is, and we believe either can revise the geas." He couldn't fully tap into the power yet because our bond wasn't complete, and my cheeks warmed at the announcement.

Khade put up a privacy spell around the two of us and leaned over to look into my eyes. "That wasn't a statement to pressure you or convince you we need to complete the bond. I meant what I said last night. It's simply a fact that I won't have control over it until we do. Just as you won't grow in power until our magics merge. We aren't rushing anything, Lyra. There are a lot of ways to combat this that don't require us having sex."

"You believe it will work, though? And so does the High Priestess?"

"Yes."

I bit my lip and tried to ignore the others around us. They couldn't hear what we were saying, but it was obvious what we were talking about. We would eventually complete the bond anyway, and even though I was nervous, the benefits of not putting it off weighed heavier on the side of "why wait". I didn't want any part of our relationship to be pragmatic, but we were facing the unexpected, and having advantages over them couldn't be denied.

Nodding to myself, I sat up straighter. "We should—"

"No." He reached out and put his finger over my lips. "Our connection will be based solely on the two of us. Nothing else, understand?"

It was what I truly wanted, so instead of trying to convince him or argue the point, I agreed, and he dropped the spell.

"So, the High Priestess believes that by pulling from Khade's ability and weaving it into the geas, his sensory or paralysis magic will cancel out Axel's invisibility?"

"After bolstering it with his lie detection, yes, since essentially Axel's invisibility is 'lying' to your senses to make you believe he isn't there," Baba explained.

"My truthsayer will detect the 'lie', and the sensory manipulation will allow us to see through it," Khade added.

Baba nodded. "It's a very complicated spell and highly theoretical, but if Khade and the High Priestess can pull it off, it will be one for the record books."

"Everyone will see through his invisibility power while we're under the geas, then?" Vale asked.

"No." Baba shook his head. "Only those within your bond group, and likely only those who've completed the bond," he added ruefully. "Through the bond, you're connected to each other on a deeper level. While direct access to each other's powers isn't possible, the bond will allow you to see through Axel's invisibility because of his lingering connection with Lyra. If it's severed, your ability to see through his concealment will also be lost. Khade would still likely be able to detect him, if not see him altogether, but the rest of you would no longer have access. Which is obviously not useful since Khade is the hidden mate and Axel only follows Lyra."

"So the geas won't reveal just anyone using invisibility, then, just Axel?" Vale clarified.

"Correct. That likely isn't ever going to be possible. This is only plausible because of the connections and magics at play through Lyra." Baba's face tensed as he explained, and the room seemed to grow quieter.

Next to me, the temperature fluctuated, chilling around Khade while growing hotter near Vale. Even the room's light dimmed imperceptibly as my mother's power slipped in reaction. An uncomfortable giggle bubbled up through my lips even as my chest tightened; my emotions seemed to shift in tandem with the ambiance of the room.

"His power grew even though he rejected me?" My eyes swam as my voice quieted in disbelief. "He benefited from something that nearly broke me?" I laughed, though it wasn't funny. I might have come to believe he wasn't the evil villain in my story I'd once thought him to be, but he'd still broken my heart and caused me pain.

Vale moved my chair and lifted me to his lap, securing me to his chest as he held me tight.

"I'm okay," I muttered, relaxing into the warmth and comfort of his arms.

"I'm not." He kissed the top of my head. "None of this will ever be okay, Lyra, but we will always have each other." His hot breath whispered into my hair. I was sure everyone could hear him, but his words were just for me, and I appreciated the reassurance. It was easy to forget that the betrayal wasn't mine alone, and I needed to remember that not only did it belong to my entire bond group, but it was especially difficult for Vale.

"We're uncertain if the ability progressed because of the bond, pumpkin," Pai tried to mollify the question that had hung in the air. "Regardless, it seems likely that his talent has developed, and we're taking precautions, assuming it's true."

"His Divination is listed as Affliction in his records, and we only know for certain about his telekinesis. With Vale's account of him using an invisibility talent as a child, it could have matured on its own," Baba tried to reassure me. But the words were out there, and they wouldn't have said them or agreed to bring it up unless it was likely true—Axel's power had grown because of our connection, however fleeting and broken.

I hadn't even known that Axel had telekinesis; I'd only been aware of his imperium earth talent and fire magic. I wasn't sure how I felt about the possibility of him having invisibility. Or him using it to follow me around. I didn't feel like he was a danger to me, but that didn't mean I wanted him surveilling me, watching me from the shadows, or eavesdropping on my conversations.

"If he is using it, would he have heard anything he shouldn't have?" I sat up with a start. "If he's been trailing us, he could have heard something."

"No, Lyra." Father's voice was louder than my worry. "That would have been one surefire way to know someone was listening who shouldn't be. The geas would have prevented you from saying anything. It has a protection spell that senses Divination magic in use around you for that exact reason. It wouldn't be a very effective tool if someone could simply camouflage themselves and get information about the hidden princess."

My mother smiled at me. "Think of yourself as safe as this castle. All the security measures that have been woven into the Night Court for eons, and have allowed us to continue as we do, are part of that geas that protects your identity. We might not have always been able to add a loophole into the binding magic, but it's an intelligently crafted spell."

I relaxed at her explanation and ignored the list of questions my mind was trying to dredge up.

"The High Priestess said she needed time to work the magic, and we still require a sample of DNA from Axel." Baba looked at Vale. "That task is easiest for you to accomplish."

"It won't be a problem."

"Good. Then, until we have something more, Lyra, you'll need to continue on as you have been."

"It might be worth considering having Lyra study from home." Khade drummed his fingers on the table. "With the new portal gates, we could easily stay at our cabin in the Winter Realm. Caldor is working on installing the same enchantments as we speak. When he's finished, it will be as private and sealed as the dorm. Perhaps better, since no one will know we are there."

My parents looked at each other and then back at us after a few moments. "Given the new information, we don't disagree, but we'll leave that up to you and your mate to discuss and decide on," my mother said.

Vale snorted and rubbed my back, but he didn't voice whatever he thought was funny. When I looked at him, he just gave me a wink.

The three of us left shortly after, and as soon as we were in the dorm living room, Vale spun around and scooped me up, so I wrapped my legs around his waist.

"I have to go, but I'll be back for dinner. If the boss doesn't have plans, I'll bring home pizza." He tipped his head toward Khade with a teasing grin.

Khade walked past us, taking his suit jacket off before draping it over the back of a chair. "If Lyra wants pizza, get pizza."

Vale waggled his brows and asked Khade if he had any requests before setting me down.

"Whatever you choose will be fine," Khade replied.

I wrinkled my nose and looked at him. "Vale likes pineapple on his pizza."

His head snapped up to Vale with barely contained disgust. "A supreme will be fine. Thank you."

I giggled at his change of order, and when he looked down at me again, his eyes twinkled with amusement. His features barely changed, but I was learning to read him and could see the humor in his eyes.

After saying our goodbyes, I closed the door behind Vale, turned to Khade, and squared my shoulders. "I don't want to leave."

"We're going to the cabin," he said at the same time, then tilted his head and crossed his arms over his chest. "This isn't negotiable."

Chapter Eight

My eyes widened. "Excuse me?"

"Lyra, the evidence speaks for itself. Axel is a safety risk to you."

"I don't believe that."

"That's because you're kind and want to see the good in everyone," he stated, coming to stand in front of me. "I may not have known you for long, but I've figured that much out about you already."

"He's had ample opportunity to harm me, and he hasn't. He protected me in Cobalt Mountain."

"And yet he's following you around like a stalker under the cloak of invisibility." His gaze was heavy as he stared at me. "I'm not in the business of compromising the Night Kingdom's safety—and you are the Night Kingdom, Lyra. There's no room for error."

"I understand, but my opinion should be considered, and my judgment factored in." I tried standing taller, but even with him crouched, he towered over me.

"Alright. I can be reasonable, little mate." He smirked, trailing his finger up the front of my throat before wrapping his hand around it—like he'd done the first time we met. "If you want to negotiate, present your case," he whispered over my mouth, then flicked his tongue out to trace my bottom lip.

Well, that backfired because now I couldn't think, let alone speak. A whine slipped up through my mouth as I squeezed my thighs together. Khade hummed at the sound before sealing his lips against mine. Wrapping his free arm around the small of my back, he stood and lifted me to him, so I did what my instinct desired and wrapped my legs around his waist, settling my aching center over the bulge in his trousers.

Threading my fingers up into his short midnight hair, I was rewarded with another throaty grumble as he walked across the room. I expected him to sit in the chair or take us to the couch, so when the cold, hard surface of the countertop met with my ass, I was surprised.

He released his hold from around me, and then faster than I could track, he had both of my hands behind my back and secure in his grip. Slowing his kiss, he pulled my bottom lip through his teeth and then scattered love bites along my jaw until he reached my ear.

"I'm going to ask you questions while I touch you. Do you consent?" His cool breath tickled a sensitive spot on my neck as his kisses whispered over my skin with barely there touches that made my stomach clench in desire for more.

I nodded almost frantically, but he tightened his grip on my hands a fraction, and then I remembered how he liked my words.

"Yes," I gasped, my shirt stretching tight as I panted. "I consent."

"Good girl." The bass of his voice vibrated through the hold he had on me. When he pressed his lips against my pulse again, it wasn't the soft whispering kiss from before; they were hard and heavy, full of tongue and teeth.

The hold he had around my neck loosened as the pads of his fingers drifted over my skin and down between my breasts.

His baritone voice was rich, filling my mouth. "What is your favorite color?"

My brow creased. The question was not what I'd expected and so off topic I thought he was joking, so I didn't answer.

But then he stopped.

He stopped kissing me. His hand on my chest stilled. Even the grasp he held around my wrists seemed to suspend, though his grip never lessened.

"Black," I blurted, instantly rewarded with a soft press of his lips.

"Violet," he answered in return.

His questions stayed simple for a while: my favorite flower, food, movie, song, and book. Then, the required answers increased gradually from one to two words to short sentence responses. *What does my perfect day look like? Where is somewhere I've always wanted to go but haven't?*

Staying in, wearing pajamas all day, and eating my favorite foods in the bath were similar to his casual day of reading and no electronics. But while I wanted to visit Pearlmoor Citadel in the Starlyn Sea, he wanted to travel to Altairia Skye, the floating resort city above the clouds.

With each answer, his touch grew in pressure, but it never eased the tension; instead, it built it. He trailed a finger between my breasts, circling but not touching my nipples before sweeping under the soft tissue. Running his hand down my side, he dipped a finger between the waist of my jeans and over my hip bone before massaging my thigh.

When he finally released my wrist, he told me not to move, then fisted my hair and kissed me hard as he laid me down on the counter. After letting loose the strands, he flicked his tongue out to lick my lip's edge, tracing the bottom so delicately I shivered.

"Who was your first kiss?"

The question pulled me out of the moment, and I shook my head. "I don't want to know your answers to those questions," I admitted.

He stopped instantly, placing his hands gently on my face to hold me while he looked down at me. We stared at each other for a few quiet seconds, and then he gave me a nod. "Then I won't answer them."

He didn't know everything about Axel or the parts that involved Jana, but I could see the understanding in his eyes. In this case, jumping to conclusions was an accurate leap.

I wouldn't typically be jealous of previous lovers, but I'd heard so much about Khade already, and after everything I witnessed and heard between Jana and Axel, I wasn't comfortable enough to know these things about him yet.

"I'm not insecure about your past, Khade, but I don't want the finer details." I couldn't have those swirling around in my already overactive mind.

"Any time you feel this way, tell me immediately, like you just did. Your safety in all facets is my top priority, understand?"

"Thank you." My eyes wanted to prickle, but I fought against it.

"Will you still answer for me?"

My cheeks warmed. "That doesn't seem fair."

"I've not gone through what you have, so it won't bother me and I promise I won't be jealous—especially not of boys." He leaned over me, caressing my face as he kissed me sweetly. When he broke the kiss, he looked at me with reverence, revealing a piece of his soul. "I want to know everything about you, but I need you to know: I've never shared anything meaningful with anyone. I've let no one in the way I will you. I've never been on a date, made public appearances with someone, or allowed anyone to step foot into my personal spaces. Not my homes, not even my office. All of those have been reserved for you. You're the only one I've ever truly wanted, Lyra, and other than the rumors you've heard, there is zero evidence to the contrary. I made sure of it. We are forever. You have nothing to fear with me."

My heart swelled so much it threatened to burst from my chest, and despite my efforts, tears escaped my eyes.

"Khade..."

"I want to know everything about you, including the parts of you I dreamed of having for myself." He took my hands and lifted them over my head. "Will you tell me your secrets, little mate? Will you share with me your memories and experiences from your past?"

"Yes," I granted his request.

Khade dragged his fingers down my raised arms sensually, and when I tried to ball my fists to stop myself from squirming, I found I couldn't move. I didn't know how he was doing it or with which power, but my arms wouldn't budge, though I could still feel them. I sucked in a breath. My eyes widened with his smirk.

"Now, be a good girl and tell me what I want to hear," he crooned, running the pads of his fingers down my chest and over my nipples.

It was the first time he'd truly touched me, and I felt my panties dampen with the tease, and when his pupils dilated, I grew wetter with his exaggerated inhale.

When I shared the story of my first kiss, Khade insisted on more details, and after I provided them, he refined the memory. He held me where I'd been held and pressed our lips together with cautious and curious sweeps of his tongue, as if tasting me for the first time. It was sweet and tender, filled with chaste excitement. I would always remember my first kiss, but I was certain that if I ever thought of it again, the echo in my mind would be overshadowed by Khade's emulation.

"How were you touched here?" he asked, cupping my breasts as if with tentative curiosity. "Was the first time over your shirt?" He palmed the soft tissue and squeezed gently, testing. Then he thumbed over my nipples again, and I moaned like a wanton virgin. "Like this?"

"Yes." I panted as I tried to push up into him for more.

None of my firsts had ever been this exciting, and I was more frustrated now than I had been then. Now, I knew what I liked and what I wanted; then, I'd been curious and hadn't known what to expect.

He teased me over my shirt for a while and then slipped his hand under the fabric as I described my memory to him. A deep groan rumbled at the contact of bare skin, but his focus never wavered. Lifting the tee, he exposed me to him for the first time, and every nerve in my body came alive under his darkening gaze.

"Please..." My clit throbbed as I whined. Forgetting our game and impatient at the play, I hoped his control would slip with mine.

I was too hot, or the air was too cold, but the temperature made me tremble. I still couldn't move, and his control over my body had spread down to my undulating hips and thrashing legs. The restraint both tantalized and thrilled me further.

"Did he kiss you here?" His voice was throaty and deep as he bumped his fingers over the hardened peaks of my breasts. "Did he put you in his mouth and taste your creamy skin?" He seemed entranced as he asked, almost like a plea, and thankfully, I could answer him with a yes.

"Yes. Please, yes. He sucked on them."

Khade's patience seemed to know no bounds as he slowly and lingeringly laved each nipple, circling the peak and flicking it with his tongue. When he finally pulled one into his mouth, I nearly came. He hummed in approval at my reaction, and with the rumble that vibrated the sensitive tip I knew it would take nothing but the briefest touch against my swollen flesh to give me a reprieve.

The questions continued with each teasing touch, switching back and forth between general topics about my past and skirting around the original subject of staying at the cabin. I'd agreed to always put my safety first and detailed my first date, then conceded to the convenience of the new portal gates after telling him about my time spent with Sidric.

I was writhing and whining as he made his way down to my navel before stroking his tongue back up over my breastbone. Then, to my absolute horror, he lowered my shirt.

"You're perfect," he whispered over my cheek, peppering me with light kisses. "I can't wait to hear the rest of your stories, love."

I wanted to cry out in exasperation, but he kissed me hard and shut down any protest I might have made. When he pulled away, my lips were wet and swollen, and I was breathing so loudly I didn't hear the door open.

"If you're going to tease her, Khade, at least have the decency not to do it while I'm training," Vale grumbled, slamming the door and stomping over to the counter where I was still laid out like an offering.

"I'll try to keep that in mind. However, take this as a sign to practice your mental boundaries." Khade's voice was less bothered than it had been moments before as his cool demeanor slipped back into place. But when he looked down at me, I could still see the fire in his eyes. "Take care of our little mate while I'm gone. She deserves a reward for being such a good girl."

Chapter Nine

The next morning I was still coursing with pent-up ecstasy, even after the half dozen orgasms from Vale the previous night.

When Khade released me from his hold and before he even left through the portal, Vale had me stripped and in the shower with him, and just as I'd imagined, as soon as the head of his fat cock touched my swollen flesh, I cried out in relief even as I clawed at him for more.

I slept like the dead and felt great this morning, but after breakfast, Khade resumed his coaxing and teased me into compliance before sending me on my way. By the time he was finished, I had promised to spend the day gathering my assignments and informing my professors that I would work remotely for all the classes I shared with Axel, essentially accounting for my entire week. That left me at school for only two days, with the rest of our time spent at Khade's cabin.

It was entirely too easy to give in to him and his terms. The prospect of him touching me was like a thirst I needed to quench, and he wouldn't give me a drink until I agreed. It was one hundred percent coercion and not a compromise, but even now, I couldn't find any annoyance about it to care.

Was there a downside to spending alone time in a remote cabin in the middle of the forest with my mates? I couldn't think of any.

I was a little sad to learn that Callie wasn't here, but when she told me she and Jed were with their new mates, I tried to pry as much information out of her as I could through text. She was being tight-lipped, which was unusual for her, but she told me their names were Elle and Atlas, and they both worked in the medical field. She seemed extra excited about that, so I was equally giddy for her.

I was more than a little distracted walking into my econ class, but I felt the moment Axel's eyes locked onto me. He was leaning against his table when I came in, and when our eyes met, he moved as if to approach me but stopped abruptly. He seemed to visibly waver, holding himself still as his eyes roved over me, almost as if looking for something out of place. When his gaze finally landed on my face, he searched my features, but it was me who discovered something unsettling within him.

The blue of his eyes was so much brighter against the bloodshot red of his normally white sclera. The soft tissue under his bottom lid was dark and sunken. His pallor was dull and gray, and though I couldn't be certain, he appeared to have lost some weight.

I stepped forward to ask him if he was alright, but he simply offered me a faint smile before turning to slump in his chair. The way his shoulders sagged and his head hung sparked a pang of worry within me, but as I moved closer to reach him, Professor Warrock smoothly intervened, blocking my path.

"Good morning, Ms. Bruadar. Did you have a nice weekend?" He smirked at me in that mischievous, flirty way that I was positive was just his personality and not an actual interest in me anymore.

"Weekends are always nice, Mr. Warrock. How was yours?"

"It was a non-starter, unfortunately," he muttered beneath his breath with a shrug.

It was safe to assume from his remark that he'd been hoping for something more during his professional attendance at the Winter Revelry. I didn't know him well, but it was an easy conclusion to jump to. After all, Axel was the only person I'd ever known to actively avoid his fated mate. Everyone else seemed happy with the prospect. That little reminder didn't erase the pang of concern

I felt at the sight of Axel's disheveled state, but it was enough for me to abandon my desire to check on him.

Professor Warrock made idle chat as he walked me to my seat, and soon after, he called the students to attention and went into his lecture. The lesson consumed most of the class time, but after assigning us tasks, he made his way to my side of the room and took the chair beside me—a spot he seemed to favor.

We sat quietly for a few minutes when he surprised me by putting up a privacy spell.

"How are you really, Lyra?" he asked, his voice low but laced with concern. "We didn't get a chance to speak at the ball. That was your first revelry since..."

He didn't finish the sentence. He didn't need to.

At first, I was confused by his question. But I quickly remembered it was because he didn't know I'd found Khade. No one did, and no one could. So, I had to play my part. As much as I hated the idea of deceiving everyone, especially those who had done nothing but support me and have my back since before they found out about everything, I held onto the hope that they would understand when the time came for them to know.

Resting my head on my hand, I sighed, which wasn't forced at all. It felt wrong to lie, so instead, I skated around the truth and leaned into the discomfort of dishonesty. "I'm not disappointed. Vale and I had a great time, and it was leaps and bounds better than the last revelry I went to." I snickered so he knew I was truly okay.

He chuckled, and I was glad to see the smile he gave me reached his eyes. I was hopeful our burgeoning friendship wouldn't suffer from my omission.

"Self-deprecating humor is a language I'm fluent in." He winked. "You and your giant mate looked as though you were enjoying yourselves, but if I'm being honest, I was surprised the dragon could move so gracefully."

I laughed at him. Vale was a very good dancer, and I'd be lying if I said it didn't surprise me a little too. "I felt like a streamer to his baton as he twirled me around."

"I'm certain his quick step will help him on the field too." He nodded.

"What about you, professor? I saw you dancing with a few ladies."

He smirked. “Don’t worry about me, sweet dream. My time is coming soon, but I know everything will work out in the end. Besides, I’m still hopeful.” His eyes twinkled, then he looked away to pull in an exaggerated breath. “In the meantime, I’m single and ready to mingle.”

I blurted out a laugh and cringed at the terrible line. “Oh no, please don’t say that. It’s awful.”

He chuckled, and when he got up, I told him I’d be working remotely for a while. He didn’t question it and instead agreed to send over the next several assignments so I could keep myself busy.

After he dismissed class, I caught sight of Axel heading in the opposite direction from normal, when my sudden concern for him irrationally took over again, so I went after him.

“Axel.” My voice wasn’t loud over the clamor of students, but he stopped instantly anyway and turned to face me.

His brow was furrowed, but his eyes were curious and wide as he watched me approach him with rapt attention. With each step I took, his breathing grew slow and heavy, almost anticipatory.

There was something eager in the air between us, and his obvious attraction to me wasn’t something I could ignore. But there was too much chaos between us, and the satisfaction I felt from his lingering gaze was as deep as I was willing to explore the feeling. So I pushed it away and focused on his ailed appearance.

“Lyra?” His voice was gravelly and worn, and his brows pulled down in confusion at my approach.

“Hey.” I smiled.

The action appeared to puzzle him more. His head tilted in inquiry, but his lips lifted, mirroring my own.

“Hi,” he said, then we stared at each other a little awkwardly for a moment until he cleared his throat. “Was there—”

“Are you okay?” I put a hand on his arm and felt the muscle twitch under my touch. He was warm, almost feverish, and I wondered if he really was sick. “Are you unwell?”

He sighed and closed his eyes briefly, then shook his head. “I… No, why?”

His tone wasn't snarky or accusatory, just baffled. We weren't friends; we were barely acquaintances, and by all rights, he should be my enemy—the last person I wanted to engage with. But he didn't know what I knew. The notion that he might actually be a victim played in my mind, and an urge to ensure his well-being stirred within me.

I hesitated for a moment before answering him honestly. "You look tired. Are you feeling alright?"

A huffy laugh escaped his lips. "No. I'm not alright, Lyra, but I'm dealing with it. The best I can." He gave me a somber smile.

"Do you need help? Is there something I can do?" I blurted out before I could stop myself.

So many things swept across his features in response; I swore I felt them. Hope, remorse, a plea, want, and desire before dejection and brittle disappointment that seemed to physically weigh down his already slumped shoulders.

"There's no going back now, Lyra." He shrugged like what he said wasn't that big of a deal, but the defeat he was displaying said the opposite. "I... I just haven't been sleeping well, is all."

I knew he was lying. We both knew it. If he was referring to what had happened between us, then he was correct—what's done was done. And if he was alluding to his potential involvement in things I wasn't supposed to know about, then the die was cast for that too.

I squeezed his arm before pulling my hand away. "If you ever need anything, Axel, Vale is around. You can call him."

"Yeah," he muttered, flicking his eyes away from mine. It was then that I noticed they lacked their usual spark, even with the sun shining on his face. During the times he was pushing me away and being cruel, his eyes had held a glimmer of vitality, but now they just seemed dull. When he looked at me again, his expression was resigned. "I'll see you around. Take care of yourself."

"Get some rest, Ax—"

The heat from a wall of roaring flames blew my hair back with the force of its intensity. Fire crackled through the air as the acrid scent of smoke filled my nose and choked my lungs. Horrified screams were an undertone to a clamor of chaos, confusing my senses as uncertainty gripped my mind. An instant of eerie silence blanketed the unknown before it too was shattered by a resounding boom, followed by a blistering whoosh of torrid air that dimmed all other sound.

Axel's arms were around me in the next second, and acting on instinct, I opened my magic up to him, bolstering his power as he threw up a wall of loam between us and the inferno—encasing us in a natural shield of rock, dirt, and clay made by his elemental expertise.

The turbulent commotion cut off as abruptly as it had begun, and where it had been blinding a moment ago, it was pitch black and silent now.

The air in the earthen dome was stifling, and the smell of burned hair and fabric overwhelmed the small space that should have only smelled of soil. Without my magic, I couldn't see in the inky darkness of the barrier Axel had created, but drawing from the power of his wolf's eyes, they glowed enough to faintly light up our surroundings.

"Lyra, are you hurt?" he demanded, wrapping his hands around my face before running them over my body as he looked me over.

I couldn't see him very well, but I felt when his shirt fell off in tatters to land on the ground. "I'm fine, but you're not!" I screeched as the unmistakable scent of burned tissue and blood reached my nose. "Axel!" I pushed his hands away, and without overthinking it, I pressed my palms against his bare chest and impelled my magic to heal him.

"Lyra..." he huffed, tensing under me as I ran my hands over him.

I didn't know what I was doing exactly, and the only time my mate healing had ever taken over was when Vale came to me with busted knuckles. Thankfully, my instincts knew what to do, and a few moments later, he relaxed under the glow of my mending.

"Thank you." He slumped forward, releasing the whispery words in an exhale. I had no idea how bad the damage was, but the smell of charred flesh told me everything I needed to know about his pain.

"Are you okay?" I gingerly moved my hands from his front to his back. If he wasn't fully healed, I didn't want to hurt him, but I needed to know if his burns were knitted together or if I should push more of my power into him.

The muscles under his taut skin twitched under my touch, and tiny bumps raised under my fingers as I skimmed over his skin. I lightly brushed my hands over his shoulders and the spine of his neck before reaching around him, under his arms, to feel my way down the length of his back. I moved slowly so as not to hurt him, gently grazing over the sculpted expanse. When I reached the waist of his jeans, I found the fabric there singed but still mostly intact. Left behind was a dusty charcoal layer that felt grainy against my skin as I brushed it away. If his pants had been made of a lighter material, he'd probably be naked and not just shirtless right now. The thought jolted me out of my unconscious examining, and I jerked my hands away from him.

"Sorry. I just wanted to make sure you were healed." I tried to look anywhere but at him. Unfortunately, there was nowhere else to look—he was all around me as we stood encased in the small, dark space together.

"You don't have to apologize for touching me." The glowing blue of his eyes was brighter now. "Ever," he added when I looked up at him.

The energy spiked in the room to such a degree that a sudden and intense pull between us made me stumble a half step into him until I was pressed against his entire body. His arms wrapped around me, pulling me tighter to him, and he rested his forehead against mine.

"Lyra..." he crooned as the temperature rose and our breathing sped up. "I—"

Muffled screams and sirens vibrated through the terra walls around us, stiffening us both and sobering the mood. I backed away from him as much as I could, which only left inches but was still much-needed space.

"We need to get out of here." I cleared my throat.

Without a word, Axel removed his arms from around me and pushed against the dome, pressing his palms against the hardened dirt, looking for weak spots.

"If you're willing, I could use the help to get us out of here. I don't know what happened, but this is solid, and I don't know if I can break us free on my own."

He rapped his knuckles against the wall, emphasizing his point. The sound was a dull thud, like knocking on concrete.

"Is the fire gone?" I put my hand on the formation to see if I could feel any heat. I didn't sense anything with my elements, but neither of us had sensed anything before it happened, and we were nearly burned to a crisp because of it, so I didn't exactly trust my instincts right now. Plus, Axel was half naked in front of me, and the fragmented mate bond that pulsed between us wasn't helping to keep my mind clear.

"May I?" He held out his hand for mine.

I was eager to be out of here, so when we made contact, he grunted at the touch of my insistent magic that spilled into him. The intensity of our powers mingling made my stomach clench, and I wondered what it would feel like to do this at full strength. Or during sex. With him.

But that was stupid and never going to happen, so I shut that thought down before the next thing to scent the space around us was my arousal. I could hide a lot of things from him, but that wasn't one of them.

"The fire's not out, but it's not raging like it was." He was breathless when he spoke, and I dared not reply for fear of sounding just as excited and turned on. "I'm almost certain it's safe, but..." He hesitated, looking down at me.

"But what?" I whispered.

"But I'm not positive." He reached out and pulled me against him again, wrapping his larger body around my smaller frame. "Stay close to me," he ordered. It was so different from the cautious way he typically spoke to me that it took me off guard, and the bossy demand for my protection had me holding back a needy whine. But then I realized what he was saying, snapped out of it, and yanked my magic back.

"I'm not using you as a shield!" I pushed at his chest. "You were already burned once, protecting me. You're not doing it—"

"I'm not risking you getting hurt, and I can be healed," he snarled and tightened his hold on me. "Don't argue with me."

I tried to push him away again, but when he wanted to be, he was as solid as a brick wall and just as unyielding.

"Power share with me." His voice was low in my ear. "We need to get out of here, sweetheart. We're running out of oxygen."

Huffing in irritation, I rolled my eyes so he would see before opening my magic up to him again. "Don't call me that," I grumbled instead of moaning and rubbing myself on him.

"Feisty." He chuckled, but before I could push him away again, he pulled on our combined element and busted through the solidified earth.

I ducked my head, hiding from the dust and debris, and ended up with my face buried against his chest—his warm, naked, muscular chest that held the faint scent of spring, pine needles, and rain. When the air was clear and bright around us, I stepped back so quickly he had to steady me so I didn't fall.

By the goddess, what the hell was wrong with me?

When I was secure on my feet, I moved away, distracting myself as I dusted off and looked at anything but him.

The quad was scorched. Where there was once lush grass, bushes, and trees, there was now smoldering bark, smoking branches, and charred land. Yet the burn looked intentional. All around us, there were spots of green, and the way the singeing was spread out, the damage to the trees looked like accidents caught up in the branding.

The crying and shouting were only dulled by the alarms coming from the buildings. Students and staff were running around, helping those who were hurt and using whatever magical ability or element they could to stop the flames and control further damage.

"We need to get you out of here." Axel grabbed my arm and pulled me with him as he walked in the opposite direction from the destruction.

"No." I tried to remove myself from his grip. "We need to help—"

"You're not safe here, Lyra!"

"Axel…" I tried again to stop him, but he didn't relent.

"I'm not watching you get hurt again. You either walk, or I'll carry you. It's your choice, but you're leaving—now." His steps were wide and hurried, and I practically had to jog to keep up with him.

"You're not—" I stopped mid-sentence as we came around a corner. "Professor Farellaw!" I shrieked.

Axel released me at my determined approach to my political science instructor. She was trapped under a large branch that was still attached to a burning tree, its leaves falling around her as they withered and died from the fire's searing heat.

"Lyra..." She looked at me with a whimper, followed by a sharp intake of breath. "I can't move... The pain..." She shook her head. Her legs looked broken, and the exposed flesh around the injury was blackened, burned, and bleeding.

Reaching out with my earth, I tried to shift the tree, but there wasn't enough life left in it for me to access and manipulate its essence in order to guide it away from her.

"Axel?" I looked at him for help as he knelt beside me.

He gave me a single nod before turning his gaze down to meet hers. "I'm going to sift the earth and build it up under the tree to slide you out. Neither of us can heal you, though," he told her.

"It's okay." She gritted her teeth. "Just do what you can, it's still ... burning." Her voice was tight as she panted through the pain.

I felt so useless. I couldn't even extinguish the fire. Even if I wanted to out myself with a water ability, there wasn't anything close enough for me to draw from. The fountains were empty, and the pipes underground that fed the sprinklers and the buildings were dry; the only water source close enough that I could sense was the sweat on each of our brows, and I couldn't do squat with it.

"Ready?" Axel asked her once he was in position.

I stood behind him, trying to give him room while also keeping my hands on him and my magic open for him to draw on.

When she gave him the go-ahead, Axel sifted the ground around her. The earth shuddered, and Professor Farellaw let out a yelp of pain as the soil enveloped her. As she sank into the crumbling ground, the tree rose off her, balancing on two mounds like a bridge. When she was free from the trapping, Axel slid his arms beneath her body and pulled her away from the danger. She lost consciousness when he lifted her, and once the ground was stable, he moved her to a safe distance.

I tried to wake her after he laid her down again, but she didn't stir. She was alive. Her breathing was steady, but the wounds were worse than I had imagined. Both of her legs were crushed and covered in what appeared to be second-degree burns.

"She needs a healer. I can stay with her."

"I'm not leaving you," Axel stated, but when I raised my eyes to him, his attention was on his phone.

"Axel, she needs—"

"I said I'm not leaving you." His eyes were hard when he met mine. "Something is wrong here, Lyra. The campus is unsafe, and I'm not letting you out of my sight right now. Help is on the way. There was an alert sent out. A healer will attend to her, and Professor Farellaw will be fine." He turned his phone so I could see the notice that had been sent out to all students and staff, instructing them to find a safe place and share their location if someone was injured—which he had—before stuffing his device back in his pocket.

"You saved her." I caught his eye again and, as if on cue, she stirred and moaned in pain, proving she was still alive, all thanks to Axel.

"You're safe. Someone's on their way to heal you," I reassured her, taking her hand in mine, attempting to comfort her.

She nodded at me, sucked in a breath, and looked up at Axel. "Thank you," she croaked, grimacing through the pain as her eyes swam with gratitude.

He didn't say anything to her, but moments later, we were surrounded by help and healers.

We stepped back to give them room, and when I went to remove my bag to grab my phone and let everyone know I was safe, Axel wrapped his hand around my arm and moved us away again. "Let's go."

"Axel—" I started to argue, but my protests were cut off with a roar—a deafening roar from a dragon in the sky.

Vale soared overhead, his powerful wings cutting through the air in a wide arc as he circled above. His sharp eyes swept the landscape, his movements deliberate and focused as if hunting for prey. The instant he spotted me below, his flight abruptly shifted, and he tucked his wings as he nosedived straight toward us.

"What the hell is he doing?" Axel pulled me next to him before tucking me behind his body as if to shield me from the fierce dragon hurtling in our direction.

Vale roared into the sky once more before his feet touched the ground—and without missing a beat, he transformed into a giant naked man, charging at me with determination—with his massive dick swaying and slapping against his thighs.

Chapter Ten

I watched in pure fascination as Vale's muscles moved and contracted with each step he took toward me. My cheeks warmed at the sight of him—tall, strong, and glorious—and if anyone other than Axel had been paying attention to him, I would have been jealous of them seeing what was *mine*.

"Vale..." I grunted when he swooped me into his arms and crushed me to him. His skin was hot to the touch, and he was breathing heavily, but it didn't stop him from inhaling my scent like I was the oxygen he had been deprived of.

He held me securely against him for a moment before he pulled back to look at me, moving his hands over me the same way Axel had right after the attack happened.

"Are you okay? Are you hurt?" His worried eyes roamed over where he hadn't touched me yet. "Do you need a healer?"

"I'm okay." I grabbed his face between my palms. "I'm fine, I promise. Why are you naked?"

He grunted, and instead of answering me, he kissed me possessively. Vale plundered my mouth and held me steady to take what he wanted—what he needed from me—and I willingly and gratefully gave it to him. When he broke the kiss, he moved his lips across my face, over my cheeks, and along my jaw.

"There wasn't time. I was training when I heard the alarms, and when you didn't answer your phone, I took to the sky. My gym clothes aren't spelled for a shift," he said between the pressing of his lips, then pulled me against him again, where he buried his nose in my hair.

"We should do that later." My voice was strained from the pressure he was holding me with, but I was equally happy to be wrapped around him and decided that I could live with limited air as long as I was safely in his arms.

"Why?" He pulled back to look at me, and the confusion on his face made me snicker at him.

Axel snorted too. "So you don't scare the locals with your monster cock the next time you shift."

Vale ignored him, rolling his eyes as he took in the scene around us. "I can't tell if it looks worse on the ground or from the sky. I need to get you out of here in case this isn't over."

As much as I wanted to stay and help, I knew he wouldn't let me now that he was here. Khade would lose his mind if he did, and I was sure my parents would forget I was an adult and try to ground me if I tried. There were already tons of people on the scene helping anyway, and I'd just be in the way since I couldn't fully access my magic.

Plus, he was naked.

"Okay. Are we going on foot?" I eyed him up and down before looking down at my shirt, pulling at the hem.

"No," He and Axel said in unison at my silent suggestion. Vale even reached out and pulled my hands away from the fabric to smooth the tee back into place.

"You can't walk around like that!" I protested.

"You're not taking your clothes off, Lyra," Vale growled and tugged on the bottom of my shirt again like the mere thought would lift it over my head. "Axel can make me a loincloth out of grass or something."

"Seriously?" Axel raised his brows at him like he was joking. But he clearly wasn't.

"The Night Guard are on their way, and the quad is swarming with people—students, staff, and help from town. I shouldn't stay nude, and you don't have spare clothes to share, so unless you want her walking around campus without a shirt…"

Axel turned on his heel and jogged over to a felled tree that was smoldering but no longer on fire, and he grabbed a handful of branches. By the time he was back, he'd created a type of jungle thong made of twine that was layered with oversized leaves.

Vale grinned, taking it from him with a little too much enthusiasm, and stepped into the creation. He tucked himself into the cupping leaves and tugged the sapling twigs around until they were settled on his waist. He shimmied and shook his hips, then jumped up and down a few times.

"I look like Blaine of the Rainforest." He hooted.

Despite the suffocating gravity of the situation, I latched onto the glimmer of humor and chuckled at him and his silliness. It was a horrible time to make jokes, but the brief escape offered a momentary break from the turmoil.

"You look ridiculous," Axel deadpanned, and I had to cover my mouth to stop from laughing.

Vale put his hands on his hips and opened his mouth, but a surge of activity caught our attention.

I turned to the rising smoke from the smoldering flames in the distance, and my heart quickened as familiar figures emerged, moving through the area with purpose and determination. The sight of my parents and brothers arriving, accompanied by a contingent of Night Guard trailing behind them, lent an air of security to the scene that promised relief. I instantly felt more at ease knowing the threat would be met head-on and defeated now that they were here.

My breath caught when I saw Khade beside them. His face was set in a hard mask of urgency as he scanned the quad, his presence commanding and fierce as he swept his gaze over the destruction like a gust of wind ripping through trees. When his eyes met mine, a sense of danger lurked behind his calm mask, but nothing that frightened me. Instead, the connection that stretched between us comforted me, even as a clash of emotions contorted his face. But he didn't move. His fists clenched, his jaw locked, but his feet stayed rooted next to the Queen—a cold reminder that, even amid chaos, we had a role to play.

His intense gaze held me in place as he looked me over, scrutinizing every inch of me while my bond thrashed in my chest, urging me to go to him and comfort him as a riot of emotions slammed into me from where he stood. I wanted to spin so he could see I was fine or whisper words of reassurance to him that all was well, but I couldn't, especially with Axel by my side.

When his gaze finally left mine, his face pinched at the sight of Axel before landing on Vale. They held each other's stare for a few seconds, and whatever was unspoken that passed between them had Vale straightening his spine as a renewed sense of urgency came from him through our bond and into me.

"The cavalry's arrived, so we should go." Vale turned and knelt down so I could climb onto his back.

Axel nodded, holding his hands out as if to guide me or catch me if I slipped. "Where are you going to—"

"What are you doing here? I thought you were leaving!" Professor Warrock appeared suddenly, cutting off my view of my family and Khade, and looking me over frenetically. He glared at Axel, then at Vale, throwing an order at my dragon mate, "Get her out of here, now!" he hissed, which made me wonder what his shifted form was.

"Already on it." Vale hiked my legs up, gave him and Axel a curt nod, then sprinted in the opposite direction.

I turned to look at Axel to say ... something, but Professor Warrock snapped at him. "Axel, you're with me." He waved him along as he jogged toward where my family was taking action.

As I held Axel's gaze, hoping to convey my gratitude for his repeated acts of saving me, he dipped his head and offered me a reassuring smile, just as Vale turned a corner and disappeared from view.

When we were back in our dorm, he didn't pause or let me down, and instead took us to the closet, where we stepped through one portal and right into another.

I expected to find myself at home in the castle, but the room was unfamiliar. As Vale made his way down a dark hallway, my breath caught at the sight of a spacious and open room. Oversized furniture filled a huge living room, featuring a sectional sofa accented with pillows and plush throws, surrounded by recliners, and anchored around a glass, wood centerpiece table, and side stands.

The rustic walls were tall and peaked, holding floor-to-ceiling windows that looked out onto a picturesque view. Past the wraparound deck and in every direction was a wintry forest of snowy mountains and frosted trees. A light pattering of snow fell gently from the sky, hushing the realm around us in quiet comfort, blanketing the world in a serene, ethereal beauty.

Even as the soft flakes danced in the crisp wintry air, inside the room was cozy and warm. A massive stone fireplace, with walls of river rock and a mantle made of thick plank wood, filled the home with warmth from a roaring fire as crackling flames heated the space.

The scene carried through into the state-of-the-art kitchen, and it was so beautiful that I couldn't find the words as I looked around in awe.

"Is this the cabin?"

"Yes." Vale slipped me off his back and turned to wrap me up in his arms. "The castle was safe, of course, but this is—"

"Perfect." I tried to peer around his shoulder to keep looking at the beautiful home, but he was intent on capturing my full attention.

"Are you sure you're okay?" He frowned with worry as he looked me over again.

"I really am. I promise." I stood on my toes and tipped my head up to kiss him. "Why are we here?"

"When you weren't answering your phone and before I shifted and left everything behind, Khade sent me three words. 'Find her. Cabin.' I was already aiming to do the first, so I brought you here. Do you have your phone?"

Nodding, I shrugged off my bag as I headed into the kitchen. When I pulled out my phone, I was met with a low battery and a long list of missed calls and unanswered messages from everyone.

The group message with my family was a mess. Callie's were worried. Vale's were frantic, and the four I'd received from Khade were demanding.

KR: Lyra. Tell me where you are.

KR: Answer me.

KR: Lyra, tell me you are safe right now.

KR: Respond.

I took a picture of the view from where I was and sent it to him.

Me: I'm safe.

His response was immediate, like he was holding his phone, waiting for me to reach out to him.

KR: I will be there shortly.

I took a picture of myself and then one of me and Vale and sent those too, just because. Then I responded to the others, checking on my family and making sure Callie and my friends were all in one piece. When I finished, I handed my phone to Vale so he could reach out to his family, and after making a quick call to his parents and his sister, he pulled me against him again.

Wrapping my arms around him, I let myself melt into his embrace. "Why does this keep happening?"

"I wish I knew." He kissed the top of my head and rested his chin there. "Why didn't you answer your phone?"

"There wasn't time. Everything was chaotic. We'd just left Professor Farellaw when you found us. She was hurt badly, and Axel saved her. I was going to call, but then there you were." I smiled, remembering what he was wearing. When I pulled away to look at him, I couldn't contain the laughter I'd held back earlier. He really did look ridiculous. It didn't help that he banged on his chest and bellowed into the air like the cartoon character from our childhood.

When he swept me up into his arms to kiss me, I hoped that everyone else who'd been caught up in the attack would soon feel as safe and loved as I did at that moment.

When he put me down, he took my hand and led me down another hallway, peeking his head into each room and closet we passed by. It didn't feel right wandering and snooping through the rooms of Khade's home, but Vale didn't seem bothered, and when we came to a room that looked promising, he didn't waste time going through the drawers to find something to wear.

"These will work." He lifted a pair of plaid lounge pants, pulling at the waist and stretching them as far as they could go. After nodding to himself, he looked me over, then dug through the drawer again. With a t-shirt and a pair of boxers in his hand, along with the pajama bottoms, he pulled me into the ensuite. After ripping off the twine and leaves loincloth, he promptly stripped me out of my smoke- and smut-filled clothes and turned on the shower.

I wasn't sure how often it was used, but there were full bars of soap for our hair and body, and after we were cleaned and out of the spray, we both smelled like Khade. Which was nice—at least for me—and smelling Khade on Vale's skin mixing with his scent did something to my insides that made me squirm.

"Now I want to wash you with my soaps." Vale smirked at me.

I'd been sniffing my hair after drying off, and I knew I had a silly smile on my face. "I smell like you all the time." I blushed, dropping my wet hair to get dressed.

"Do you smile and blush like that for me too, my sweet mate?" he whispered over my cheeks.

"You know I do." I captured his lips and let him lift me to him, where I wrapped myself around his body.

Instead of giving in to lust, we managed to control ourselves and went back to the kitchen, where we made tea and Vale raided the cupboards and refrigerator for something to eat. He was always ravenous after he shifted, and I was glad there was food in the house since we didn't have an endless buffet for him to gorge on like we did at Araphel.

As he shoved stacks of cheese and crackers into his mouth while making a sandwich, I put two frozen pizzas in the oven, then pulled out a third and made a salad.

Vale finished his first sandwich and was biting into a second when the thudding of footsteps drew my attention to the hall. Khade rounded the corner, tossed his suit jacket over a chair, and marched up to me. Grabbing the back of my head, he crushed his mouth to mine and pulled me close to him, trussing me around him.

"When you didn't answer me, I..." He clenched his jaw.

"I'm sorry, everything happened so fast—"

He cut me off with another kiss. "I'm not angry with you. I knew you were alive," he said, pressing his hand to my chest where I could feel a glimmer of him in my bond. "Tell me what happened."

He took my hand, and the three of us went into the living room. I told them every detail I could think of from the moment I'd left class. I knew Khade especially didn't like or trust Axel, more than anyone else in our inner circle, but I believed he was innocent of the attack.

"He's not that good of a liar," I told them when they both stayed quiet after I'd defended Axel's innocence. "I don't know him well, but I've had time to study him. He wasn't faking his surprise. He wasn't prepared for the attack. Not specifically, at least."

"What do you mean, not specifically?" Vale's brows pulled down.

"He always insisted I needed to leave Araphel. But I don't believe it was because he knew that this would happen. He warned me away, but I don't believe it was because he knew there'd be violence, not like what happened. He didn't hesitate to help Professor Farellaw, and he protected me. Again. He doesn't want me hurt."

Vale relaxed with my answer and nodded. "I agree." Khade glared at him, but he held his hand up and continued. "Listen, man, I might still be on the fence with his involvement in some of this regarding the NNC, but not when it comes to her. He's a prick, he did what he did, and he regrets it, but being involved with anything that might hurt her..." He shook his head. "There's no fucking way he'd do that. Not after Cobalt Mountain, and especially not after the honey incident."

"Which he was indirectly responsible for," Khade ground out through his teeth.

"I know." Vale's voice was hard as he stared him down. "But you didn't see the fear in his eyes or hear the terror in his voice when he recounted the story and thought he was watching her die. That alone is why I don't believe he'd hurt her."

"Then get proof. The crown can't take your word for it alone, and neither can I. I don't know him beyond what's on paper, and even though I believe you because I know you're not lying, there needs to be evidence to back your claim." Khade went to the drink cart and poured himself another three fingers of amber liquid. "This is three times she's been hurt or near hurt while he's been at her side. Once might be an accident, twice could be a coincidence, but three times is a pattern." He turned, looking at me as he slipped one hand into his slacks while bringing the crystal glass to his lips. "Regardless of all that, you're staying here until there's proof that he's not a danger to you."

I stood. "Khade, you can't just make that decision."

"I haven't." He squared his shoulders. "I won't lie to you, Lyra. I agreed with your mother and fathers, but ultimately they've decided. You won't return to Araphel until we are certain what side of this line Axel stands on."

Chapter Eleven

I was annoyed and pensive for the rest of the night. Khade took it in stride and didn't act any differently, not that he had a lot of free time to dote on me or discuss the decision to keep me here further. He'd barely informed me of the ruling when his phone rang. He looked as frustrated as I felt, but he left me to my thoughts and went back to work.

I discovered through my pacing around the house that his office was next to the room he'd put the portal in, and I'd heard him coming and going, back and forth through the night until I finally fell asleep next to Vale on the large sofa.

Vale was my consummate support and tried to soothe me. He even attempted to get Khade to reconsider his position and speak with my parents. When that didn't work, he went to the castle himself, but it was no use. Once my parents decided on something, especially when it concerned the safety of the Night Kingdom or their children, they rarely changed their minds.

I felt like a child who'd been given permission to do something and then scolded when they'd done it. What was worse was I couldn't even vent to my best friend about it. Our phones weren't secure enough to discuss anything, and even if they had been, I couldn't tell her about Khade—which was what I really wanted to discuss. Informing Callie about my parents' decision to keep me home wasn't unusual, and I suspected a lot of other students would be in a similar situation, so the venting for that was pretty unsatisfying. And discussing any of this with my summer sunshine supportive mate wasn't the same. I finally gave up looking for an outlet and just buried myself in a book until I fell asleep and woke up in bed moments ago.

Vale was snoring next to me, his heavy arm draped over my side with me tucked against him as the little spoon. I enjoyed his comfort for as long as I could ignore the bathroom, but once I was up, I went in search of my winter mate.

Even though it was the middle of the night, the house was as bright as the sun at noon, and the smell of coffee was thick in the air. There was a flickering coming from the living room and a low hum I assumed was a television, while quiet voices in conversation filtered down the hall from Khade's office.

His door was cracked, and when I pushed it open, a low whine came from the hinges, drawing his attention to me. He held out his arm, beckoning me toward him, so I padded quietly across the room. As I approached, a smooth, deep voice emanated from the speaker, and I strained to focus on the information being reported. The voice was distracting, a velvety-rich sound that captured my attention more than the crucial information on which I should have been concentrating.

"I need to call you back," Khade interrupted the man and my sudden fascination.

The speaker must have been accustomed to Khade's abruptness because he simply agreed with a single word and ended the call.

"You should be sleeping." He stood and pulled me against him.

"You need rest. Why are you still up?"

He tipped my chin up and smirked down at me. "I don't seem to require as much sleep as you."

I felt my cheeks warm at his teasing attention, and he chuckled softly as he bent and kissed each one.

"Are you still upset with me?" he whispered over my face. His cool breath hinted of whiskey, reminding me of rich leather—refined and polished. I wanted to taste it on his tongue.

"Not exactly." My voice was thready as I moved to capture his lips.

When I brushed my tongue across his bottom lip, he groaned low before wrapping his hand around my throat to plunder my mouth. He pulled at my lips and swept his tongue against mine until I was keening.

"Tell me." He spoke around my bottom lip before pulling it through his teeth.

I was breathless, and my mind was muddled when I blinked up at him. "What?"

"Tell me why you're upset."

Sighing, I rested my hands on his face, wiping away the wetness from his lips while I took a moment to collect my thoughts. I understood why the decision to keep me safely tucked away had been made, but ultimately, it came down to one simple thing.

"My entire life has been decided for me, my every choice predetermined by the happenstance of my birth. I've been concealed from the world and controlled entirely by tradition, by my parents ... and now by you."

He seemed to stop breathing, and his body became rigid around me. He stared at me unblinking, and then without taking his hands off me, he removed his hand from around my throat to gently pull me into an embrace. "I'm so sorry, Lyra." He sighed into my hair, slowly tightening his hold on me with each word. "I vowed to surrender my allegiance to you, and I've failed to do that."

"You haven't failed, Khade." I held him close.

"I promised to stand beside you, yet I've stood in front of you. I'm not used to not getting my way. My actions have proven that and worse, at your expense."

"I know you did it to protect me. I understand and agree with our customs. I know the geas limits my abilities, and even without it, I'm not at full power, but..."

"But you deserved a choice in the matter."

I nodded. "And if I'd been given one, with more information after what happened today and considering your wishes, I likely would have agreed anyway. But I wasn't considered or even consulted for my opinion."

His eyes softened, and the kiss he pressed to my forehead held a touch of sadness. "Your agency matters to me, Lyra. I don't want you to believe that it doesn't. I should have spoken with you before standing with them. I let fear for your well-being override my judgment and place by your side. I will do better." His voice was firm in determination.

"We're still learning, Khade. I don't expect you to be perfect, and I'm not naïve enough to think that building this bond and life together won't come without bumps in the road. Just as I know we won't always agree or share the same perspective on other matters."

He pulled in a breath and stared down at me thoughtfully for a moment before responding. "There are many things I want to lead you in, but your autonomy is not one of them. Promise me you'll always come to me if I overstep."

"I promise." I lifted on my toes to kiss him. "Now, come to bed."

He smirked, shaking his head as he attempted to argue. "I can't..."

"You need rest. You haven't slept for days. Even a river needs to bend, Khade." He ran his fingers down the side of my face, but when he didn't immediately agree, I pulled a page from his book and used coercion and begging. "Please. I want you next to me."

I squeaked a little in surprise when he swept me into his arms. He was quick to click off the lights and, in a few strides, he was walking us down the hall and into the room. "That will not work every time."

"As long as it works sometimes. I like to get my way too." I beamed up at him.

"Noted." His eyes sparkled with playfulness as he pulled back the sheet for me, and as I lay in bed, I shamelessly watched him undress down to his boxers.

With Vale sound asleep next to me, Khade pulled me against him, easily tucking me into his side, where I used his chest as a pillow, and we each fell asleep quickly.

When I woke the next morning, I was alone but cozy with both sides of the mattress still warm. I was torn between staying between the sheets with the scents of Vale and Khade surrounding me, or getting up and seeing them in person. Both were irresistible options, but in the end, my morning breath and growling tummy decided for me.

After freshening up, I noticed an open door in the room I hadn't paid attention to yesterday. Curiosity got the better of me, and when I looked inside, I was wide-eyed in disbelief.

The room was half the size of my dorm back at Araphel, split into five sections with one full of clothes I recognized. Pieces from my room at home were scattered among new items that still had tags.

"I hope you don't mind." Khade's voice startled me, and I spun around to find him leaning against the door frame, one foot crossed over the other. The top two buttons of his white shirt were unfastened, and the sleeves were rolled to his forearms. "I had some of your belongings brought from the castle." He nodded to the closet behind me. "Then I took the liberty of hiring a personal shopper to curate additional items for you, using the ones I had provided as a reference."

"Why?" I was dumbfounded.

He wrinkled his brow like what he was saying should have been obvious. "Because this is your home and you should have some of your things here."

I looked back at the closet, then at him again. "How did you have time for all this?"

"A perk of long waking hours." He smirked at my obvious dismay before leaving me alone. "Get dressed and come have breakfast before Vale eats it all."

I was ... giddy. I wanted to squeal, but they'd both hear me and that was entirely too embarrassing to risk. They'd also know if I put up a privacy spell so I was stuck containing myself in faux maturity and settled instead for smiling at fabrics and jumping up and down as quietly as possible while looking through the hangars and drawers.

Everything was well suited for the winter realm, and although there were a few pretty dresses, the closet was mostly filled with all the comfortable things I liked. The sweaters were oversized and soft, there were plenty of relaxed jeans and stretchy leggings, and a drawer full of fluffy socks that made my toes happy just thinking about.

The knit dress I wore over thick tights went down to my knees, and as much as I wanted to put on the boots that matched, I opted for slippers since I wasn't going anywhere. After I finished combing through my hair, I tried to calm the frenzy of butterflies in my belly and wipe the smirk off my face before leaving the bedroom, but it was difficult. The thoughtfulness of Khade ensuring my comfort while we stayed here made me feel seen, especially after feeling overlooked and unheard yesterday.

In the kitchen, Vale sat at the counter with two plates of food and had bitten into half a slice of toast when he spotted me. "Morning," he mumbled around a smile, then shoved a heaping forkful of scrambled eggs into his mouth.

"Are you still starving?" I raised a brow at him. This was more than usual for him. Normally, after shifting, we spent extra time in the dining hall so he could eat his fill, and sometimes we'd even take extras as carryout, but it never continued into the next day.

He grunted. "I was shifting and running drills yesterday before all hell broke loose. Then, when I went in search of you…" He didn't finish. He just shrugged and crammed two sausages into his mouth. I didn't think he even chewed fully before he washed them down with an entire glass of orange juice and took another bite of toast.

"Don't choke," Khade warned him, handing me a cup of something warm as he ushered me to a chair.

"I can eat a cow whole in dragon form; pancakes and eggs aren't a problem." Vale lifted said pancake with his fingers, rolled it up, and bit into it like a burrito after dipping it into syrup.

"I hope you don't act like this in public," Khade grumbled.

I smiled at them, settling into my seat and taking a sip of coffee from my mug.

"How did you sleep?" I asked Khade as Vale grabbed another pancake and rolled it around sausages—this time, before eating it.

"I've never slept better." Khade kissed my temple.

After Vale finished consuming enough groceries for a family of four, he excused himself, only to return a few moments later, dressed in workout clothes with a bag in hand.

"Where are you going?" I didn't mean for my voice to sound panicky, but it did.

"Overnight training." Vale scooped me into his arms. "Don't worry, my mate. I'll be back in a couple of days."

"A couple of days? What do you mean, overnight training? Why am I just learning about this?"

"After yesterday, with everything that happened..." He paused and looked at Khade. "I need to be prepared. Training with the Night Guard was always part of my duty as a Knight, and I don't want to wait until graduation. I want to learn, and I need the practice to be competent in a fight or defense of you."

"You are though. And your shifted form is a dragon..."

He shook his head. "That's not the same, my sweet mate. I can't always be a dragon, and if I need to protect you, our family, or anyone else, I want to be capable of doing it without magic or relying on my shifted form."

"But won't that cause suspicion? You've never had an interest before."

"No." Khade shook his head, answering my question with more information than I'd thought to ask for. "After what happened yesterday, there was an influx of enlistment requests. As unfortunate as it is, it's good timing for us, and because of that, Vale's decision won't spark any question. He'll just be one more among the masses."

Vale made a noise before setting me back down. "I doubt Irondale would agree."

"Just play your part, Vale." Khade's tone was bored and castigating.

I looked to Vale for an explanation. "My trainer was confused about why he was being asked to train me specifically, and that was before it went from three days a week to six. If anyone will have something to say about my enlistment, it will be him."

"He'll get over it," Khade said dismissively. "He's one of the best, and he'll do his job. Taking flak from your superiors and fellow trainees is part of the experience."

Furrowing my brows, I glanced between them. "I'm still confused."

"Requesting a Captain as my trainer is 'privileged', and it was relayed that I 'demanded' to be trained by the best. Since I'm friends with a Night Duke and I'm a noble son, I was given preferential treatment." Vale sneered.

"Oh." I pinched my lips.

Vale hated being treated differently, and while he'd threatened to use his family name and connections for me when he thought I needed his influence, he didn't want it defining him. He was humble and wanted to earn his achievements by merit, not entitlement, and throwing his position around was not in his character.

"Who put in the request?" I frowned. I knew he wouldn't have, and by his obvious discomfort, he didn't appreciate it either.

"I did," Khade said. "The request came from me, but attached to his petition request was a letter from Vale's father and a letter of recommendation from Puck."

"How did you get him to do that?" I was surprised.

Khade shook his head. "I wrote it myself and had him sign it. Puck runs on his clock, and I'd prefer not to waste time."

That was true, and I was positive Puck was fine with getting out of work while receiving all the praise.

"He thought it was hilarious until your mom put him and Roko in the same training class." Vale chuckled. "He complained the entire time yesterday."

"Oh no." I pinched my lips to hold back my laughter at my brother's expense, and I cringed for the trainer who would suffer along with Vale and everyone else in the class now.

"Yeah..." Vale dragged out the word before kissing my cheek and setting me down. "It's why I know Irondale will have plenty to say about it. It wasn't just me who used nepotism to pull a high-ranking captain from his regular duties to train a bunch of noble heirs, but now he has to put up with the biggest brat of them all."

"Is your trainer really that bad?" I was a little worried now—not for his safety, obviously, but about the punishment in the form of training he might have to endure for it.

"No, not at all. He's cool. He's a hard-ass and kind of cocky, but..." Vale shrugged. "He just isn't a fan of privileged nobles taking advantage. Which isn't hard to understand."

"Do you have to train too?" I asked Khade, worrying my bottom lip, wondering how much time I would spend here alone. If I were at Araphel while they were doing all this, it wouldn't be so bad. At least I'd have my classes and Callie...

"No," he interrupted my spiraling thoughts as he moved around the kitchen to clean up the breakfast mess. "I underwent training years ago. After graduation, I enlisted with the Night Guard and worked my way through the program while interning under your father at the castle."

"Showoff," Vale grumbled, but it sounded more like a tease than him actually feeling put out.

I smiled at Khade when he looked over at us. "That's why you don't sleep."

Khade ignored Vale to smirk at me. "Staying busy is exactly why I don't sleep. And doing both is why I'm in the position I'm in now." He looked at Vale. "I trained alongside Irondale. He's arrogant because he's that good, and his shifted form is equally impressive. It's why we all agreed that he should be the one to train you. If Lyra wasn't under the geas and under threat, she would be right beside you."

"Pass. I don't want to do that." I wrinkled my nose and picked at the fruit on my plate.

Realistically, I understood the importance of being trained to protect myself, but the idea of fighting someone was highly unappealing. The things I still had to learn to do with my magic before ascending the throne were bad enough; I didn't want to add physical violence to the list.

"None of us want that," Khade said. "But if this situation isn't resolved before your remaining mates are found and your identity is revealed to the realm, you may need to consider it."

"By whom? I'm not good at push-ups, and working out makes me stink!" I was being a princess about this, and I knew it, but I didn't like physical labor. I liked books, flowers, and pretty dresses. Not running and sweating. Gross.

Khade's irises blew wide at my complaining, and Vale smirked as he ran a hand down my back, placating me.

"Irondale is the best." Khade cleared his throat. "It's likely he'd be the one to train you."

I huffed.

"It won't be that bad. Really, he's just cocky because he still has fans from his glory years as a Starball champion. You two will probably get along fine." Vale grabbed his bag and slung it over his shoulder.

"He couldn't have been that good. I've never heard of him," I grumbled and took a bite of strawberry.

Vale snorted. "He played for Ebymm Academy, and you're biased." He kissed my cheek.

"All the schools are equally great."

"Spoken like a true Queen of the Night Kingdom. Don't forget about me while I'm gone." He winked, then disappeared down the hall.

"They are all great." I shrugged to myself and pushed around my eggs. I could believe that and have a favorite team. Just because I hadn't heard of him didn't mean anything. "Are you leaving too?" I asked Khade as he rinsed his cup.

"No." He looked down at my plate. "Are you finished?"

"Yes." I quit playing with my fork and instead helped him clean.

When everything was in order, he held his hand out for me. "Come with me. I want to show you something."

Chapter Twelve

"What is this?" My eyes widened as I looked around the room. There was so much, and I wanted to soak it all in.

In the dimly lit space, a cocoon of comfort enveloped me. There were no windows or art on the walls, but every nook was filled with cozy luxury, offering a retreat to lose myself in. A selection of plush blankets, varying in texture and color, were strewn around the room and draped over the sofas and chairs. Scattered on the furniture were plump pillows in an array of shapes and sizes, all in soothing, neutral tones that looked soft to the touch, and at the heart of the room was a bed so massive it could easily fit multiple people.

It was a haven of tranquility.

"It's your nest," Khade answered me quietly, his cool breath easing down my neck as he spoke next to my ear. "It's temporary if we should need it until you can build your own."

Why would I want to do that?

"It's perfect." I shook my head, dismissing the idea. I couldn't contain myself any longer and drifted around the room, touching everything—marking it as my own.

There were no scents here, other than a hint of Khade. Everything else was clean and odorless. Past the massive bed was a partition wall with a spa bathroom, and on the opposite side of the room was a small kitchenette. I ignored them both in favor of running my fingers over the furniture, pushing my face into the pillows and hugging the blankets to my chest, petting them like they were soft, furry creatures. I didn't feel compelled to scent the bed since I wasn't experiencing my heat, but everything else in the room was fair game and I made sure to perfume it all.

When I passed in front of a mirror and caught my reflection, I realized my wings had unfurled and were trailing behind me—smoky tendrils spread out as they slid over the space, touching and scenting every surface I'd missed with my hands. I was happy and content in a way I'd never thought to be before, and the little purring, chirping noises I couldn't contain were an indication of that.

Once I finished, I turned to Khade as a different determination filled me. His eyes tracked my movements with rapt attention, and there was a satisfied serenity in his features.

I was in front of him in an instant, wrapping myself around him as he caught me in his arms.

"You like it, little mate." He didn't so much ask as state the obvious.

His voice was low and guttural, and I was already wet and needy, but feeling the vibration of his words between my thighs had me mewling.

I couldn't speak, not really. My mind was muddled with joy. "Yes..." I whimpered as I kissed him, devoured him. "Please..." I felt like I was begging, but he was already moving, leading me away from the nest we would use someday. My first heat cycle wouldn't occur until after all my mates were revealed to me. It could happen weeks, months, or even years from now, and until then, the nest would remain unused.

But his room was ready now, and so was I.

In our room, Khade stood me on the bed, wrapping his hands around my face. "From the moment I met you, there was no going back, Lyra. But I need you to tell me this is what you want, that you're ready to complete the bond."

"Yes." My voice was breathy, but full of conviction. "I want this. Please... I don't want to wait anymore."

Khade's pupils dilated before turning into slits. He slid his hands down over my shoulders, trailing his fingers over my chest and down my hips, before grabbing the hem of the sweater dress and pulling it off over my head. The bra was less lucky as he tore the delicate fabric between his fingers before slinging it across the room.

"You're so beautiful." His voice was like satin when he spoke the words.

He didn't break eye contact as he dispensed with my panties, pinching each side and tearing them as easily as paper. Then he slipped them through my legs, slowly, and the lace teased over my sensitive flesh, making my nipples pebble and my breath hitch.

"You remember what I told you?"

A whimper slid up my throat as my voice quivered. "Yes."

Holding me steady with his eyes, Khade unbuttoned the cuffs of his shirt before rolling the sleeves to rest under his elbows. His movements were paced and deliberate, and my stomach clenched in anticipation. When I pressed my thighs together, Khade's nostrils flared with his inhaled deep breath.

"You're wet for me, love." His voice was low.

I trembled. "Yes."

"Let me see."

If I hadn't been studying him the last week, I might have thought him bored. He was so calm and controlled. But I had been watching him. The way his eyes would slightly flare when he was aroused. The practiced and steady swallow and deliberately even breaths he would take when things were excited between us. There was an obvious difference between his natural, commanding confidence versus when he was trying to hold himself poised and in control. The way his eyes darkened and his pupils slit weren't the same as his calculated stare. The subtle differences that I'd learned to recognize emboldened me with confidence.

I knelt before him, attempting to mimic his calm, but I was coursing with adrenaline and anticipation, and shook to hold myself steady. Sucking in a breath, I lay down. I'd never been watched like this before, and I hesitated for only a second before I let my legs fall open.

The air was cool against my wet heat, and the temperature difference tingled against my clit.

"Good." His voice deepened to match his breathing, and his breaths grew shallower as he finally let his gaze trail down my body.

His eyes drank in each of my breasts, tracing one in a circular view before sweeping across my chest to do the same to the other. His perusal felt like a physical touch, and I needed more. When his eyes slipped down my stomach, my hips twitched.

"Don't move," he ordered, so I fisted the sheets and bit my lip to hold still.

I knew when his lingering stare finally reached my aching center. His pupils dilated, his jaw clenched, his nostrils flared, and he inhaled through his nose as a quiet rattle slipped up through his throat.

"Beautiful," he whispered, lowering himself until he was kneeling on the floor in front of me. Bending, he kissed one of my knees, leaving a cool chill from his lips against my heated skin, causing my nipples to pinch tighter into hard peaks. Every press of his lips along my inner thigh made me shiver, and the closer he came to my center, the harder it was for me to hold still.

Khade didn't take me with his mouth as I expected and instead blew cold, frosty air on my wet flesh; the temperature difference was so pronounced I bowed off the bed involuntarily and let out a surprised moan.

His response was a low groan, followed by a heavy hand on my thigh as he repeated the same languorous attention across my opposite leg. When his kisses reached my hip, he circled his hands around my legs and pulled me to the edge of the bed, where he leaned in and placed a gentle kiss on my clit.

"You're mine, Lyra, and this pussy belongs to me," he stated with dark eyes and deep authority.

Before I could respond, Khade closed his lips around my swollen nub and sucked me into his mouth, devouring me. He kissed me intimately, pulling, licking, flicking, and sucking until I was writhing against him and begging for more. He held me steady and firm in his grasp, my legs pinned open with his forearms, a heavy hand firm on my stomach as the other massaged my breast and plucked at my nipple.

As my pleasure grew and I tried to roll my hips chasing my release, he moved away to place gentle, placid kisses around the nerve cluster, taking away the intentional touch that would tip me over.

"Khade," I whined through my panting.

"I warned you, my love—now, you will pine for me as I did every year I endured without you." The cool breath from his words wisped on my hot flesh as his deep voice rattled the bed. His pupils slit as he held my gaze, then he dipped his head to place another light kiss on my clit before he followed through with his promise.

Over and over again he worked me up, bringing near climax before pulling away to let the excitement ease away. I was shaking and sweating, and the only thing keeping me fixed on the bed were his hands holding me down. Every nerve in my body was heightened to the room, my skin was oversensitive, my hearing was amplified, and my sense of smell was so sharp I could taste my arousal in the air.

"Please." I lost count of how many denials he'd given me as I begged. "Please... Please..." I rolled my hips again and tried to touch myself, but he captured my hands in his and closed his lips around me once more.

This time, when my orgasm rose, I expected to be let down, but a climax crashed into me so hard my voice cut off with a scream and I nearly passed out from the pleasure. Khade never relented. Instead, he hummed in delight between my legs, lapping and licking me through the overpowering orgasm.

Then, he changed tactics.

Over and over he brought me to climax, never letting me recover before he was working me up again. I was toiled and trembling, but he held me in place, his hands anchoring me to the bed as he kept up his ministrations.

"Khade..." My voice was strained as I fought against another orgasm—nearly dissolving into a fit of tears when it crashed over me once more.

When it ebbed, he finally released me, kissing my thighs as my heart beat wildly in my chest. My arms and legs slumped against the bed, and my head lolled as I shuddered and panted.

"You're perfect Lyra," he whispered, bringing my attention to his gaze again, while he very slowly pushed his fingers inside of me.

I didn't think I could take anymore, but the feel of him stretching me, even with just his hand, had me mewling for him. I clenched around him; he curled his finger and pulled against me as he kissed up the length of my body. When he reached my breasts, he gave each a thorough amount of attention before hovering his face over mine as he watched me slowly come undone. I was so stimulated and sensitive when he pushed the heel of his hand against me that I surrendered to him once more.

He whispered words I couldn't understand as he pressed kisses over my face and lips, and when I wilted into the mattress, he finally withdrew his hand from my center. I was hot, my limbs were heavy, and my pulse made me twitch as it passed through each hypersensitive part of my body.

Exhausted but still in so much need of him, I watch through blurry eyes as Khade undressed. He stared at me as he unbuttoned his shirt, and as each slip of his fingers revealed more of him to me, my core pulsed with anticipation. He tossed the white shirt onto a chair in the corner, then unbuckled his belt, dragging it through the loops before casually dropping it to the floor. His pants followed, and if he was wearing anything else other than his boxers, I didn't know since he was gloriously naked for me in the next second.

He took himself in hand, and whatever he saw on my features made him chuckle darkly. "It'll fit," he assured me with a leisurely stroke.

I wasn't sure.

He had the longest cock I'd ever seen. Where Vale's was thick with a fat mushroom head, Khade was big and incredibly long, with a head that flared wide like an arrow.

Kneeling between my weak legs, he wrapped his arm under my waist and lifted me to the middle of the bed. "You're doing so well, little mate," he commended before sealing his mouth to mine as he settled between my legs. "You're such a good girl, coming for me so prettily."

My body flushed with his praise as he ran his hands over me. When he had me where he wanted me, I lifted a shaky hand, pushed my fingers up into his neatly kept hair, and pulled on the cool locks. "Fuck me, Khade."

His eyes glowed brightly as his shifted form made an appearance. His inner lids blinked over the slitted pupil of his eyes as his skin shimmered with his obsidian color before returning to his dark tan tone.

"With pleasure," he practically purred as he pulled my leg up around his waist.

Khade leaned back, angled his straining cock down, and pushed himself into me, rocking his hips in and out until he was thoroughly coated with my arousal. He groaned with each retraction, and when I shifted in impatience, Khade wrapped his hand around the base of my throat and held me in place as he filled me up. My voice caught as I stretched deeper than I'd been before, and when I didn't think he could go further, he did.

"That's it; open up for me, little flower," he crooned and rocked forward, finally bottoming out. I relaxed once he was fully seated and moaned when he circled his hips, rubbing his pubis against me. "Look how well you take me; this pussy was made for me." He grunted, squeezing my leg before pulling out again. When he reached the end, this time, he didn't hold back when he shoved himself into me with one long, lengthy stroke. "You're all *mine*." His voice rattled with the claim as the bond took over, then we were both lost to it and the pleasure.

His rhythmic movements deepened as we united, our magic intertwining with the merging of our souls as it bound us together for all eternity. When my climax hit, it surpassed any previous experience I'd had with him tonight. The release took me by surprise as it pulsed through my entire being, stretching beyond my boundaries and pulling Khade with me. His movement stuttered as if his orgasm struck him just as unexpectedly, and a guttural groan chorused with my moan in the room. Every nerve in my body felt alive with pleasure, and when it finally waned, in its place was a powerful connection between us. I could feel his elation and utter satisfaction, just as I was sure he could feel mine.

Wrapping his arms around me, he continued to rock himself into me as the bond we shared settled and our hearts found a normal rhythm.

I ached everywhere in the very best way and was completely exhausted, but Khade was truly mine now and I was never letting him go.

Chapter Thirteen

The smell of breakfast woke me the next morning as Khade padded into the room, holding a tray of food and looking gloriously disheveled.

"Stay," he ordered, kicking the door shut before coming over to set the tray on the bed.

He looked ... captivating. I'd only seen him once without clothes on and not walking around with tousled hair and his impressive physique on display.

"My eyes are up here, mate." His voice was amused and gravelly from sleep, but he didn't make any moves to hide himself from my perusal.

"Mmhmm." I bit my lip and continued to sweep my eyes up his impressive body. Khade's towering build was toned, with long muscles, a defined torso, and obvious strength consistent with a swimmer's body. A deep V at his hips was like an arrow pointing down to his lengthy member, and I marveled at how it could fit inside me.

When I finally made it up to his face, after thoroughly checking out his sculpted chest and arms, he held a smirk that didn't match the heat in his eyes.

"Hi." I looked up at him as memories of last night flooded my mind. I felt flush, not from embarrassment but because he was incredibly attractive. He deserved to see the effect he had on me.

"Good morning." The words were rushed as he climbed onto the bed, pulling my face to meet his for a possessive kiss, which I eagerly returned. There were so many emotions passing between us, it was hard to pinpoint one — except for the overwhelming sense of satisfaction.

Scrambling to my knees, I wrapped my arms around him, running my hands up and down his back—feeling the muscles along the dip of his spine and down to his firm ass. He groaned into my mouth when I gave him a little squeeze.

"I brought breakfast," he whispered against my lips.

Shaking my head, I nudged him to sit, where I promptly straddled him. "I don't want to eat. I want you." My breathing was shallow as I reached between us, happy to find him just as ready for me as I was for him, then sank myself down onto him.

He cursed and squeezed my hips, holding me steady when I dropped my head to his shoulder to allow my body a moment to adjust. He penetrated me so deeply that if he'd been an inch longer, he wouldn't have fit, and when I ground down onto him, there was a bite of painful pleasure where he bottomed out deep inside.

Khade allowed me some control, but he didn't relinquish his dominance. He simply moved me over him, guiding me from below as I worked us both from on top.

He whispered sweet words as he suckled my breasts and kissed over my skin, each compliment urging me on and pushing me higher until I was a mewling, whimpering mess yearning for more.

"That's it, beautiful; make yourself feel good." He moaned and panted with me, his focus on me only adding to my pleasure. "Look how perfectly you fit around me; you take my cock so well." He leaned back just enough to gaze where we were joined, and the intensity on his face heightened my pleasure further. "You feel so good, Lyra. You look so pretty riding me," he grunted, spreading my legs wider over him to deepen his view.

The room filled with our sounds and heat, both of us lost to the pleasure of our intimacy as we enjoyed each other, giving and taking until the well within me was on the brink of overflowing.

"Touch yourself." His voice strained with desire.

With his encouragement and pure unadulterated happiness, I felt empowered and comfortable to give him what he craved, confident under his guidance, because as much as he directed me towards pleasure, I knew it was my effect on him that truly gave me control.

Sliding my hand down between us, I circled my clit with one finger, keeping the others curled into my hand and out of the way for his viewing pleasure.

Khade ground his teeth and tensed his stomach as he watched. "Yes, just like that," he urged, picking up his pace. "Faster, Princess. Come on my cock," he commanded, leaning forward to capture one of my breasts in his mouth.

I clenched and slammed myself onto him, sending us both over the edge.

Khade wrapped me in his arms as we rode out our orgasms, kissing me across my neck and face as I twitched over him. "You're such a good girl, Lyra. My perfect little mate."

Khade took his time with me in the shower, washing my hair and body with a sweetness that was the opposite of his normal demeanor. He kissed me gently and lingered as he took care of me, and when I returned the favor, he didn't take over. He let me wash him and explore his body without ever making it sexual.

When we were toweled off, he carried me back to bed, where we ate the breakfast that he'd made. Luckily, he'd put it on a heated plate so the fluffy eggs and pancakes were still warm.

We spent the day lazing around in the giant bed, naked and familiarizing ourselves with each other. We talked and laughed, snacked between sharing stories, and napped when we were both exhausted from exploring how our bodies moved together.

On the second morning of our time alone, we woke early to the loud commotion in the living room, followed by Vale's heavy footsteps echoing down the hall. Khade and I were wrapped around each other, stripped and snuggled up, when my summer mate bustled through the door.

"Sorry," he whispered when we both looked up at him as he tried and failed to tip-toe into the bathroom to shower. He looked like he was dragging his feet as he stumbled on shaky legs from sheer exhaustion.

The sky was barely lightening and with the curtains drawn, it was dark enough to justify staying in bed a while longer. Khade urged me to go back to sleep as he tucked me against him, holding me to his chest and resting his chin on the top of my head.

The bed jostled a short while later, and Vale's clean summer scent, along with the warmth of his body, enveloped me as he lay at my back. He slid his hand between Khade and me, wrapping his heavy arm around my middle, and buried his face in my hair.

Khade grumbled, half asleep, but he didn't move, which filled me with so much joy that I smiled to myself as I fought back the happy tears threatening to leak from my eyes. Moments later, they were both breathing heavily and lightly snoring, which was a completely reasonable excuse to fall back asleep, so I did.

What I wasn't prepared for was the vivid dream that followed.

Instead of skipping through fields of flowers made of fruit or a garden of pasta trees and saucy lakes, I found myself in a dark room, staring down at a sleeping Axel.

He looked gaunt, and even in his sleep, the area under his eyes was a deep, purplish color as if he hadn't truly rested in a week. His skin was sort of ashen and pale, but it was difficult to tell if that was what he currently looked like or simply a trick from the muted light.

The lower half of his body was covered with a silky green sheet; one leg was kicked out and hanging over the side of his bed while the other twitched under the covers. One of his arms rested above his head, fingers intertwined with a white strip of fabric, while the other was stretched out and strained, his fist balled tightly and gripping the bed linen. He appeared angry, in pain, or possibly both and his thrashing and grunting could have been attributed to either. His breathing was labored, and as I bent closer to observe, his eyes beneath his lids moved rapidly as if caught in the throes of a nightmare.

"What the hell kind of dream is this?" I muttered to myself and flopped down on the bed.

Axel's eyes flew open as he shot up into a sitting position, his startled and sickly face coming within an inch of mine; it shocked me so much that I sucked in a breath and sat up between my confused mates.

"What's wrong?"

"Are you okay?"

Vale and Khade spoke over each other as they leaped out of bed, assuming protective stances around me as their elemental powers pulled at the energy sources in the room. As if rehearsed, Khade positioned himself between me and the bedroom door while Vale shielded my side, facing the large window.

"I'm fine," I panted, pressing my hand to my heart as I tried to calm myself down.

It took them each another moment to let their guard down, but when they did, Vale climbed back into bed behind me to pull me against his chest while Khade took my face between his hands to look into my eyes.

"What happened?" His brows narrowed as he stared at me with his full, demanding attention.

"It was just a dream."

"What kind of dream?" Vale kissed the side of my head.

"I..." I deflated, hesitating and unsure how to tell them I'd been dreaming of Axel. They'd both been utterly perfect mates, putting me first in everything. They deserved my honesty. Even though it wasn't a full dream or anything pleasant, it felt unfair to keep it from them.

"Lyra." Khade sat on the bed and ducked down to put himself in my line of sight. "Tell me."

"I don't want to." I picked at the sheet and slumped against Vale. I felt horrible, like I was letting them down. Tears welled in my eyes, and my chest constricted with shame and embarrassment.

Vale tensed behind me, and Khade's hand pressed against my breastbone before he slid it up around my neck where he held me firm and made me look at him again. "Whatever has made you feel this way isn't real. You've done nothing wrong. Not in person and certainly not in your dream, if that's all it was."

Wiping away a tear, I nodded and took a shaky breath. Logically, I conceded that Khade was right—it'd been just a dream. It wasn't solely that, though, which troubled me. It was also the whirlwind of emotions tied to Axel, and fantasizing about him while I was where I was and with whom I was, that had left me feeling conflicted and guilty.

"You've done nothing wrong, Lyra," Vale repeated Khade's words, resting his head against mine.

Nodding, I agreed. I'd just need to work on getting my feelings to accept the truth. "I know."

"Tell me what happened." Khade's voice softened.

I shrugged and offered him a watery smile. I felt a bit silly now, but I blamed it on being half-asleep and newly mated—added with the mix of heightened emotions I was trying to sort out, not all of which were my own either since I'd felt them through the bond. "It was just a dream."

"Are you certain?" His brows raised as if trying to coax me into expanding my thoughts.

I was still a little raw and confused by it all. "I think so."

"We're fully bonded now, Lyra, which means your powers have grown, and dreams don't bring back echoes with them," he said, looking down at my hands that were wringing together our black sheet—along with an illusionary green one.

Chapter Fourteen

After the hazy illusion disappeared, I was mortified. But worse, a weird sense of betrayal filled me, which was incredibly confusing. Vale and Khade spent an unfortunate amount of time convincing me that I had nothing to apologize for and had done nothing wrong.

"It's perfectly natural to be drawn to someone who was supposed to be with us," Khade said. "What you've gone through is unexpected. There's nothing to learn from since, as far as we know, being rejected has never happened before. Lyra, you didn't want or ask for this, and having lingering feelings and a connection isn't a deception to anyone. I certainly don't feel betrayed."

"Neither do I," Vale affirmed. "And if by some miracle you find yourself in a position to forgive him enough to welcome him into the fold, if that's even possible, I won't feel slighted by that either."

"It's no secret that I don't like Axel, but I agree with Vale. He should have been your first mate, and as long as your safety isn't in question, how you choose to proceed with him is between you two, perfectly natural and entirely acceptable." I could feel Khade's honesty and conviction in his statement as much as I felt it in his stare. "Even if your dream had been of someone or something else, you can't control your imagination, Lyra. We aren't upset with you."

Fated mates and multiple partners could be a tricky business, but after putting myself in their shoes, I accepted the truth. Though it hadn't happened in a very long time, one of them could, in theory, have a mate of their own outside of me. I knew I wouldn't be upset about that and would instead be ecstatic for them. With that understanding, along with their reassurance, supportive words, and feelings, I was able to release all my negative emotions about it.

Once the conversation moved beyond the person I'd been dreaming about and narrowed on the encounter itself, along with the echo I'd brought back with it, theories and ideas took over our morning. Khade and Vale delved headfirst into power research, while I had an extensive conversation with my parents about the experience, hopeful they could provide information. However, manifestation magic was so diverse that identifying a specific ability would depend on how my gift progressed, and since I couldn't yet replicate what I had done, we were all left in a state of uncertainty.

The early morning slipped away, and after breakfast, Khade returned to work. As much as we both wanted to stay hunkered inside the cabin together, he had a job to do and my parents needed him. It had only been a few days since the attack on Araphel, and though he'd been able to release statements from here, he couldn't stay out of the public for long without raising questions.

The Kingdom's academies were all on hiatus, a public advisory was in effect, and the Night Guard were on constant patrol while the investigation was ongoing. It was a stark reminder of the peaceful tranquility that the attack had taken from our realm. Yet I knew it was temporary, and I found solace in that.

Callie and Jed were safe and staying with their new mates in their apartment in the city, and as stressful as the situation was, she was happy to be there. Through her, I learned that Brev had gone back home to be with his family, and Sidric was with his new mate safely tucked away at the Lunar Sanctum.

An hour after Khade had left Vale and me at the cabin, our research was interrupted by a long, exaggerated whistle as Puck walked into the living room, wandering around and taking in the wintry scene that surrounded us.

"Swanky," he drawled, acting as if he'd never seen such luxury in his life.

"You grew up in a castle." I rolled my eyes at him.

"Yeah, but my mate doesn't have a fancy cabin in the woods." He raised his brows at me like that was a perfectly reasonable explanation. "I bet he owns acres of this forest too, and that hot tub is big enough for ten—my mate doesn't own one of those either."

"I'm standing right here," Roko deadpanned.

"And I love you, but facts, babe." Puck shrugged and flopped onto the oversized sofa chair. "I don't much care for the snow, anyway. I'd prefer a beach house—ooh, or a lake house!" He beamed at Roko and batted his lashes at him. "Will you get me a lake house?"

Roko snorted and scooched into the chair next to him. "Sure. Whatever you want, handsome."

Puck squealed and turned on the TV. "I want a porch swing too. And some sort of fluffy animal that will play fetch and cuddle. But not one that drools. That's just unsanitary." He wrinkled his nose. "And a yard with a white picket fence, like in the movies. Someday, we'll have children and the nanny will need a manicured lawn to play with them."

"A nanny?" Roko raised his brows at the suggestion, and in response, Puck wrinkled his.

"Of course. You've seen what grass stains do to Starball jerseys. You don't want me to ruin my clothes, do you?"

I snorted at him. "Don't forget the diapers."

Puck mock gagged and held up his hand. "Yeah, no, I'm not doing that either. Definitely a nanny."

"Whatever you want, my love." Roko smirked at him, then turned to me while Puck's attention flopped and he flipped through the channels. "How's the research going? Have you found anything useful?"

"It's been interesting," I told him over the piles of books scattered around the table.

"That's nerd for 'Lyra is having the time of her life'. She's just downplaying how much she loves research," Puck snickered. "When she was little and we couldn't find her, all we had to do was look in the library where she'd be with her best friends stacked around her."

"That's because I wasn't allowed to have real ones," I told him flippantly, punctuating the statement with the sound of my page turning.

Puck sat up and faced me, his mouth dropping open with a huff. "Well, now it's not funny."

I shrugged. I'd long gotten past feeling slighted about not having friends outside of my brothers and the Day Kingdom heirs growing up. "It's kinda funny..."

The news announcer on the television cut off any further banter as his voice filled the room, backed with aerial footage of protesters outside the Night Court Citadel—the central hub of governance, where my parents, councilors, advisors, and dignitaries convened to discuss matters of state, diplomacy, and the well-being of the Night Kingdom.

It was a small group, but so unusual and out of place in our realm that it was headline newsworthy. The journalists reporting had mixed footage of the protesters with the vandalism they were presumably responsible for throughout the kingdom over the last week, including the fire damage done at Araphel. The campus and buildings were repaired now, but the photos of the damage would last forever. The letters *NNC* that had been scorched into the grass on the quad would forever be burned into our memories, just as the graffiti defacing the walls for their message had stained our minds.

The images of the toppled statue of the first Night Queen stood as a chilling symbol of disrespect for everything we stood for. It was a personal attack aimed at every queen and daughter before me, and I felt a deep sorrow for the women who had carried our legacy and the scorn that this metaphor represented.

As the reeling footage of destruction faded, the camera panned away from the protesters, focusing on the grand doors to the Night Court. The newscasters' voices hushed, and the sounds from outside the Citadel grew louder. Chants and chatter melded with the journalists' subdued whispers and the indistinguishable sound of camera shutters clicking.

The shifting and rumble as the sturdy doors opened felt like an attention-grabbing announcement. My heart pounded heavily at the sight of Khade leading the charge, followed by advisors and generals making their way to the podium.

For years, I had watched him address the Kingdom in his official capacity, speaking on behalf of my parents and serving as a trusted member of our government. But it was something entirely different now that he was mine. I also no longer passed off the flutters in my belly at the sight of him as nothing more than a physical attraction to a handsome male. Not now that I understood what my intrigue for him had meant all those years. It was also a little thrilling that he was still my secret.

Khade scanned the crowd with a clinical eye, and I knew in that moment that every one of the protesters would be on a watch list. They were well within their rights to protest their grievances, as long as it remained civil, but after what had happened at Araphel, everyone in the group would be under a microscope.

Once in position, he directed his attention toward the journalists, with my three remaining brothers—Shea, Tunder, and Cleon—beside him, as well as the other prominent members of the Seasonal Courts and high-ranking officials.

"Ladies and gentlemen, I stand before you today on behalf of our Queen, Knight Lords, and as a representative of the Night Kingdom. I address you today to assure you that your concerns are not being ignored and to acknowledge your right to peacefully protest your cause. We are committed to facilitating positive change, bringing forth unity with a dedication to understanding. Transparency and open discourse are pillars of our just society, and we remain constant in our commitment to uphold these values for every citizen in the realms." He paused, and with it, the realm seemed to hold its collective breath. "However, let me be unequivocally clear: violence will not be tolerated."

When he said this, he and everyone who stood with him turned to cast their gaze over the protesters. It was as if they sought to underline the statement with a practiced and united reprimand. The weight of their concerted gaze quieted the crowd, and even here, I could feel the impact of the message. It was as if gravity itself was exerting influence over the scene, and the castigating silence carried.

"Damn," Roko whispered, shrinking in his seat as if he was under fire too.

The base of my belly warmed, but for an entirely different reason, and I knew I'd failed to hide my reaction when Puck snorted and elbowed Roko to snicker at me.

I ignored them, focusing on Khade as he looked directly into the camera and continued.

"We are resolved to ensure the safety and well-being of all within the Night Kingdom. Trust that those responsible for recent events will be held accountable to the fullest extent of the law—by me personally—with the full support of the Crown, assistance from the Noble Courts, and plenary resources of the Night Guard. As we navigate these challenges, we must stand united, resolute in the face of fear or threats, unwavering in our commitment to not be swayed by unrest or those responsible for it."

His voice had dropped and held an edge when he said this, but it cleared up again as he continued.

"I address you today not only to reassure the citizens of our great Kingdom of our commitment to restoring our realms to peaceful prosperity, but also to invite the leaders of the New Night movement to engage in dialogue. We extend an invitation for you to present your perspectives in court, before the Queen, our realm's Knights, and the lawmakers of each Noble Court of our honorable Kingdom. Together, we seek a peaceful resolution and a path toward progress. Your voices matter, and we are here to listen. We firmly believe that, by coming together, we can work towards a more harmonious future for every citizen. As we proceed, it is imperative that we remember our actions have consequences, not just for ourselves but for the entire community, and we must choose a path of integrity and compassion. Thank you."

He finished speaking, and instead of staying to answer questions thrown their way, they all turned as one and disappeared back into the Citadel. When the camera returned to the studio and the broadcasters offered their commentary, Puck shut off the TV.

"That was vague, but I think it got the message across." Puck nodded to himself.

Roko's brows lifted. "What, that they should all be terrified because Khade is coming after them, personally? I should hope so. He'll get them convicted and sent to the wastelands." He shivered.

The wastelands were akin to death for the fae. The continent, jointly governed by the Day and Night Kingdoms, housed the dregs of society and was devoid of magic. The barren land had been stripped of all its power, much like those who were sent there. They were left with nothing but a shell of themselves, housed in a flesh-and-blood prison.

It was a task my parents undertook as part of their responsibility for maintaining their positions of power. They loathed it, and I knew it was a heavy burden they carried. But some people couldn't be entrusted with the abilities they possessed, and if stripping that away from them meant safeguarding everyone else from potential harm, it was a necessary form of justice.

Thankfully, the punishment was rare, with the last sentencing having taken place years ago. Currently, only around a thousand people from both kingdoms occupied that desolate expanse. This penalty was considered the most severe, akin to a half-life existence, and those condemned were destined to spend the rest of their days there with no path to redemption or second chances.

It gave me chills thinking about it. Someday, when it was my time to rule alongside my mates, I hoped never to have to mete out such a punishment. But it was a possibility, and we would all be trained to fulfill our duty. It was the true burden of the queen's rule, the gift and curse bestowed upon us and our knights, in the balance of having access to all forms of magic and finding each other through such an influential bond. Having the power to take away a fae's very essence was a heavy onus, but one carried out with pride and gravity.

With none of us in any position to solve the realms problems, we focused on the one we could—mine.

Puck and Roko joined in our research to identify my new power. Hours later, after many caffeinated drinks, mindless snacking, and reading page after page of documents, books, and articles, we narrowed it down to dream walking and projection. Now, it was up to me to test it in action.

Since Puck could fall asleep at the mere mention of a nap, he volunteered to be my subject. "Just cover your eyes if you see something you don't like, Lala." He smirked and waggled his brows before closing his eyes and promptly falling asleep.

"That's impressive." Vale looked down at Puck's snoring sprawl on the couch with surprised confusion. Then, to make sure he wasn't pretending, he waved his hand over Puck's face erratically and made some very inappropriate jokes that would have definitely sparked a reaction from him if he'd been faking his slumber.

"He's been able to do it since he was a kid," I told them once Vale was satisfied he was truly asleep. "Our parents believe it's a side effect or byproduct of his Spirit Summoning magic."

Puck's divination gave him the ability to commune with nature spirits, including those of plants and animals. He couldn't control them, but he could ask them for help, and if they were so inclined, they'd assist him. Since the power stemmed from somewhere in the veil, neither alive nor dead, and his connection to it was so strong, it made sense he could access that state at will.

Roko nodded as he stared down at his mate lovingly. "I also think his connection with spirit was bolstered through our bond from my meditative healing, but that's too logical for him. Instead, he jokes that a spirit of Liderc is in love with him and that's why he can sleep at will."

"That's terrifying." Vale's eyes widened. "Don't they appear as a dead person and fuck you to death or something?"

Roko chortled. "That's one version of the lore. I don't think he's in danger, but it does explain all the wet dreams he has."

"Ugh, gross." I covered my ears and gagged. "You two need filters. Now I don't know if I want to do this." I cringed but sat down beside Puck's head anyway, not really sure what I was doing, and put my hand on his forehead.

"Just close your eyes like he said." Roko chuckled. "If he's right and Liderc is in there entertaining him, I'm sure you'll have no problem looking away."

"Not helpful," I whined but closed my eyes and concentrated on my sleeping brother anyway. It didn't matter, though. I couldn't enter Puck's dream or extract anything from it into the room with us, so I gave up after an hour of failed attempts.

“You were asleep the first time. Maybe you need to practice there.” Puck yawned and stretched like a well-rested cat after we woke him up.

“That sounds easier said than done,” I complained while I stacked the books to take them back to the castle. “How am I supposed to do that?”

“Guided meditation. And Roko can help.” He beamed.

Chapter Fifteen

I couldn't fall asleep to try, even with Roko's help. I was too nervous about where I'd end up. Having Puck and Vale there watching me didn't help either, and knowing Khade and my family were also waiting to hear from us if the exercise worked, I simply couldn't relax.

Instead, Roko and I compared our schedules and decided he'd come over when everyone else wasn't around. In the meantime, I'd practice on my own, starting with a meditation routine prescribed by him to ease my anxiety about this new power.

With my new therapy plan settled, we turned our attention to making dinner. The sun had set, and Khade messaged that he'd be home late, so we shouldn't wait for him to eat.

We'd gone through all the easy stuff, like pizza, burritos, and mac n' cheese, and since we were all essentially a bunch of spoiled noble kids who'd never really had to fend for themselves, Roko took the lead.

"Khade had some things delivered the other day, but we've gone through all the food." Vale shifted items around in the freezer, searching for anything that we could throw in the oven, while Roko rummaged through the cupboards.

"I grew up in an ingredients household, so I can work with this." Roko nodded and started pulling boxes, spices, and canned and frozen foods out to pile on the kitchen island.

"What the hell is an ingredients house?" Vale asked.

Puck and I had no idea, so we shrugged and watched as an incoherent mass grew on the counter. When Roko had pulled everything he needed, he set us to task as he explained, "Ingredients house versus a snack house. Basically, anything we wanted to eat, we had to make from scratch, even snacks. It was rare to find a bag of chips or frozen pizza at home. If we wanted those, we had to go buy them or make them. Same with other food. My dad always made everything fresh; pasta, dough, and even bread were all homemade."

"You made your own chips?" I was intrigued. "I've only had fresh chips at restaurants."

"They're the best! Do you have potatoes?" Roko perked up while I looked around.

"No."

"Next time, then. Today, we'll make my dad's spaghetti with vegetable bolognese."

Roko instructed Puck on how to make the dough while he focused on the sauce. Vale and I cut up vegetables and made a salad, and because we had a baguette loaf, we made garlic bread too. With so many hands helping, it didn't take nearly as long as I would've expected, and soon we were all sitting around the table with bowls full of the best spaghetti I'd ever had.

"You never said Roko cooks for you," I teased Puck between bites. "This is amazing."

Puck didn't wait to answer between bites; instead, he bragged around a saucy mouthful. "He doesn't, not like this anyway. But I knew he could."

"All this time we've been ordering takeout when we could have been eating like this." Vale shook his head and filled his bowl again. "Not anymore. You're cooking all the time."

Roko snorted and shook his head. "No way. You eat too much; I couldn't keep up. Besides, I'm taking full advantage of the cafeteria while we're at school."

"Fine, but I want to do this more," Vale pressed. "You can teach me."

"My dad would be happy to teach you." Roko beamed, then told us about his dad's love of cooking, the restaurant he ran, and the dishes they would make as he grew up.

When dinner was finished and the mess was cleaned, they said their goodbyes with a plan for all things potatoes next time. While Vale readied himself to leave for another night training session, I cleaned up and got ready for bed.

"Khade will be here soon," he told me for the third time.

"I'll be fine. I promise." I stood on my tiptoes and kissed his lips. "Now go, before you're late and you have to run extra laps again."

"Irondale is a sadist." He shifted his bag as he grumbled. "I think he likes to torture us."

"Or maybe he just likes to watch you sweat," I teased him.

When he was gone, I lay in bed, eager to try some meditation, but I quickly fell asleep instead. The difference this time was that I knew I was asleep versus knowing I had slept after the fact. Normally, I dreamed in clear images and vibrant colors. They often didn't make sense but were still coherent.

This wasn't like that. I was surrounded by a blur, like my vision was out of focus. Sounds and voices around me were muffled, and it was dark aside from the hazy images and flickering lights. Shadowy movements dimmed and brightened with each passing motion, so unclear that they could have been people dancing or trees swaying in the wind as the sun bled through the leaves.

Wherever I was, I wasn't frightened and didn't feel a sense of urgency to flee, but it wasn't relaxing either. There was this odd, almost unnatural energy that made me uncomfortable as it pulsed and flared randomly around me.

Wandering around didn't do anything; it was all the same, like I was walking in circles or pacing a room. There were noises, like people talking, though I couldn't make out the words being spoken, but it sounded like there were a few.

Sometimes it was droning, but every so often, it felt harsh like a whip cracking through the air, and the atmosphere around me even seemed to flinch.

This ebb and flow continued, and I was kept in tow. After what felt like a long while, there was a sudden heightening of activity, and that's when I felt nervous. But just as quickly as it'd come, it stopped, and a comforting silence filled the space. I no longer felt rushed, like I needed to leave, but rather like I was being welcomed to stay, so I did.

I tried to look around again, but the room remained a mystery. Even reaching out to brush my hands against phantom walls didn't reveal its secrets to me. The boundary was soft, almost smooth to the touch—silky—yet substantial in its obvious strength. I wasn't trapped; I knew I could leave, but whatever this was was also holding me in place.

The more I swept my palms over the murky surface, the more a different sense filled me—one of longing and lust. The walls seemed to shudder as I skimmed my fingers over the nebulous barrier, and the more I pushed into it, the more a deep rumbling vibrated through my hands.

My breathing sped up as the façade shrank around me, almost like a hug pulling me in close, and when I pressed myself against the surface, my nipples perked at the touch. There was a gentle thrumming, almost like a groan, as the enclosure quivered and slowly came into focus.

"Lyra..."

I followed the faint call of my name, and just when I thought I'd push through, pleasure woke me.

"That's it," Khade's low timbre whispered into my ear. His breath spilled down my neck between heavy kisses as his long fingers swept through the folds of my sex, circling my clit. "Wake up for me, my love."

I'd been aroused during the dream, but waking up to Khade wrapped around me, playing with me, had me coming on his fingers the instant he pushed them inside me and pressed his thumb down on my swollen nub.

"Such a good girl, Lyra." He skimmed his lips over my jaw as I moaned and writhed against him before he took my mouth with his in a searing kiss.

Reaching out to touch him, I expected skin or boxers and instead found a dress shirt and slacks, but I squeezed his hard cock through the fabric before moving to undo the button.

Khade didn't need further convincing. He pulled his hand from my panties, then pulled them off before doing the same to my night shirt. I was naked when he stood to remove his clothes, and instead of drawing out our time in his typical way, he climbed back into bed between my legs, pinned my hands above my head, and pushed himself inside of me in one fluid motion.

Groaning with his entry, he took my mouth again while he worked himself into me. When he was fully seated, he pushed down on my hip as he circled his. "I was on a conference call when your need filtered through the bond; luckily, I was only in the next room and could answer your siren's song. What were you fantasizing about, mate?"

"I don't know." I panted, still a little groggy from sleep. "It wasn't..."

I couldn't think clearly with what he was doing to me. The way he held me, the way he moved—I couldn't focus past the pleasure.

"It wasn't what?" he prompted me, moving his hand up to pluck at one of my nipples.

"Clear." I whined. "It wasn't clear," I rushed out, hoping he'd stop asking me questions and instead focus more on what he was doing to my body.

He grunted when I clenched down on him to encourage his attention. Releasing my hands, he trailed his fingers down my sides before wrapping both hands around my waist to leverage me. Lifting me slightly, he timed his push and movements with his opposite slide in and out of me.

"Try to remember." His voice was heavier to match his hard thrusts. "Tell me what you saw, and I'll let you come on my cock."

"Or what?"

"Or I'll make you keep coming until you do."

Both propositions sounded like a reward, and they were, but I was already so wrung out from the dream walking, failed attempts from earlier, and the orgasm he'd already given me that I didn't think I could handle his pleasure dominance right now. So I closed my eyes and tried to recall the details.

It was difficult.

He kept changing his tactics and positions, spiking the pleasure and speed, only to find that perfect spot and slow down, dragging it out. It took much longer than it should have to recount what I could remember, and when I finally got to the end, I was as sated and limber from the workout as I would have been if he'd just given me multiple orgasms.

When he finally gave me release, I was still shuddering under him when he found his, and when he carried me to the shower, he had to hold me up under the spray because my legs were like jelly.

Back in bed, I quickly fell asleep again, but if I dreamed anything at all, I didn't remember.

Chapter Sixteen

Spending my days at the cabin gave me an excess of extra time on my hands. I was able to finish up my classwork much faster than if I'd been on campus, and since there was no travel time to and from classes, blocked hours for rejuvenation and meals, or social engagements, I had tons of extra time.

So with all my newfound freedom, I spent some of it practicing the meditation technique Roko had prescribed. It was helpful, but not necessarily in the way I was hoping for. I hadn't made any significant progress in controlling the dream walking, and my astral projection was still limited, but I wasn't anxious about either and took each success and failure in stride as part of my learning curve.

I was, however, getting tons of practice on my shifting, and Vale and Khade were both eager to assist.

My limitations didn't stem from an inability to take my form but rather from the challenge of calling it at will and maintaining it despite distractions. I could transform, but if I wasn't completely focused or something disrupted my concentration, I couldn't hold it—or I'd morph at inopportune times, like when I was startled.

Vale and Khade didn't have my problem and were both excellent at partial shifting. Vale's effortless ability was especially impressive given his size in dragon form. He was straightforward with his help while Khade's methods were more involved and much less modest. Vale helped me refine my partial shifting, whereas Khade focused on getting me to hold my form while being preoccupied.

I didn't know it at the time, but my first lesson with Khade and his new training technique was him getting me to repeat my dream for him. My training didn't always involve me being naked, but when it did, they were both dedicated instructors.

"No, just your hair." Vale ran his fingers over my wings until he reached my back, then kissed down my spine until I evanesced them away.

"I can't." I panted as I tried to concentrate on putting my wings away while maintaining my nightshade form localized in only my hair.

It would have been difficult at any time, but it was even harder while sitting in Vale's lap, naked and stuffed with his cock. My legs were spread, and my hands were bound behind me, while Khade teased my breasts and clit as Vale slowly rocked our bodies together.

"You're doing such a good job, love. I'm so proud of you," Khade praised when my wings disappeared. Then, just like he'd done several times before, he increased his swirling play and gave Vale a nod of approval to increase his speed.

Most of my hair was floating around us in inky black waves while I tried desperately to hold the form and reach orgasm at the same time. I was sweaty and sensitive, and it was hard not to lose focus. The pleasure they were pulling from me wasn't something I could ignore in order to concentrate solely on my hair, but each time I let my form slip, they'd both stop until I transformed again.

I was near climax once more and they both knew it, but instead of letting me peak, they backed off just enough to keep me in limbo.

"I ... can't." I whined as my nipples tightened and my breath huffed unsteadily.

"Just a little longer," Khade encouraged before taking my mouth.

Vale was struggling with me, and with each of his groans and squeezes around my waist as he pumped himself into me, he threatened my concentration further. "Fuck. How much longer?" he panted.

"You're not the one being tested." Khade released my mouth, only to lift his free hand and run his fingers through the wispy smoke of my hair. The sensation increased the pleasure through my body, and I wanted *more.*

Clenching myself around Vale, I ground myself into him. Vale belted out as he slammed into me harder as he chased his release. Giving him pleasure would normally have brought out mine, but I wanted to succeed in Khade's instruction, so I willed myself to stay focused while rolling myself over my dragon, pushing him toward orgasm.

It didn't stop me from moaning with him as Khade fingered my hair and slipped his thumb over the sensitive apex of my sex.

"You know exactly how to make your mate feel good, don't you, love? Show me how you ride him. Make him come, beautiful," he hummed against my mouth, pulling at my lips with his teeth before kissing them between whispered words of encouragement. "That's it. You're such a good girl, Lyra."

I could hardly breathe as I focused on being just that for him.

When Vale jerked and stuttered to a stop beneath me, I wanted to weep at my success, but I was also on the precipice of failure—unless Khade released me from my restraint.

"Khade—"

He cut me off with a kiss. My voice was reedy with my plea, but he knew. He knew exactly what I was going to say, what I wanted—what I needed—from him.

His kiss was brutish and hungry, and when he took away his fingers from between my legs, I didn't have time to question him or beg. He lifted me from Vale's lap, pulling me from one straining erection, only to settle me on another.

"I've been waiting all day to put my cock in you." He groaned, bouncing me up and down his legs as he stood. "Let go. Come for me. *Now,*" he demanded. Khade wound his arms around me, pulling me down onto him as he ground himself up into me.

I didn't need to be told twice. My shifted form snapped back into the ether, my hair fell heavy against my shoulders, and my back arched at the intensity of release. My senses were heightened from the near constant edging, but more so since my cells had just re-solidified.

Khade held me through the first waves of pleasure, encouraging mine before taking his. Then he and Vale took turns rewarding me until the only thing I could do was pass out from sheer exhaustion.

Over the next several days, half of my lessons continued like this, each slightly different in technique and involvement. Sometimes it was just Khade and me, practicing in various spots around the cabin and in the woods. Other times, Vale played a central role. When Khade wasn't using pleasure play to teach me focus while holding parts of my nightshade form, they each shared personal insights and tricks learned through trial and error.

I'd been doing a magical version of jumping jacks for nearly an hour when Khade's phone rang loudly and interrupted us. We were in the backyard, which he and Vale had transformed into a private training space. Khade had melted the snow, and after Vale boiled the water with his fire to eliminate impurities, Khade shaped it into a hexagonal ice dome. Once solid, Vale dried the grass and heated the area, turning the dome into a comfortably temperate, safe place for me to practice.

"I'll take this inside." Khade's brows furrowed as he looked at his phone, his fingers tapping away rapidly on the screen.

The NNC's rhetoric and small-scale attacks had continued, and each day brought another call to Khade and reports that required his attention for either prosecution or public addressing. Although he managed to spend some time at the cabin with me, he was often interrupted and called back to work throughout all hours of the day. So, I wasn't surprised when his phone rang, but it was distressing to know that the unrest surrounding the group was ongoing. It was also frustrating because it meant that I wouldn't be returning to school anytime soon.

When Khade disappeared into the house without another word, I resumed my exercise, trusting that he would inform us of what we needed to know when the time was right. Jumping into the air, I transformed into a shadowy version of myself then became solid again just before my feet touched the ground. I was hyper-focused on my coordination to avoid losing balance when landing. I had fallen more times than I could count due to miscalculating my pace, and my knees were scuffed green from grass stains.

I shifted and reformed once more, expecting to touch the ground, but instead, I landed in Vale's arms. It startled me, but not enough to slip through his grasp in a puff of smoke, so that was something.

"Let's try something different," he said, kissing my nose before setting me on my feet. "Your nightshade's size isn't predetermined like my dragon's, right?"

I wobbled my head. "Sort of. When I turn into a specific creature, I take on their average or 'normal' size," I explained as I stretched my arms, feeling sore like I'd been lifting weights. "For example, I can't shift into a butterfly the size of a dragon, or vice versa."

Vale nodded. "What winged forms have you practiced?" he asked, wiping smudges of dirt from my face as I listed the forms I'd taken in the past.

"Butterflies, dragonflies, aphids, moths, and a variety of small birds. I haven't been able to do anything larger or more complex, like eagles or dragons."

"What about ground creatures?" He put his hands on his hips, listening intently.

"Same thing. I've done beetles, caterpillars, squirrels and mice. Once, I was able to become a cat but only for a few seconds."

"And when you're not taking a specific form and are just emitting darkness, how large or small can you expand?"

"I haven't really tried to disperse like that." I wrinkled my brow. "And my shadow fae form isn't resizable. It's just me, but in shade."

He nodded. "I'm starting to understand why it's been so difficult for you. You have so many options to be aware of and consider, aside from the power of your form," he said, as he looked from one end of the dome to the other. "Let's try switch sprints. It's a drill we've done in guard training. I can't do them with you since this space isn't big enough, but I'll run alongside you." He looked way too excited about this exercise, but I was up for any challenge that would help me control my nightshade form.

Vale demonstrated in action, shifting his wings every fifth step until he reached the opposite side of the dome, then repeated the drill back.

The first couple of runs I did, I only turned into my shadow form, so my feet were always touching the ground. After I was sure of what to do, I chose the creature form I was especially comfortable with and had spent the most amount of time practicing, which was the butterfly.

My energy was running low after half a dozen attempts, most of which were successful, even after tripping a couple of times.

I was huffing and puffing when I reached him again and took the offered water bottle from his hand. "I don't know ... how much ... more ... I can ... do."

"We need to work on your endurance." Vale waggled his brows. "The last couple, you didn't falter or trip. Are you up for a few more?"

I groaned, gearing up to pout my way out of it, when Khade hollered from near the exit. "Being tired and continuing is good practice to maintain your focus."

"You both realize I'm a pampered princess who's never had to do physical labor before, right?"

"Yes," they said in unison.

I didn't know why I'd thought whining would get me out of more laps, especially with Khade, but it didn't. Instead, he'd added a second form to the switch sprints to make things more complicated. So rather than just jumping into a butterfly between running, I was transforming from fae to bunny before leaping into a butterfly.

Too many laps later, I was exhausted, and on my last attempt to jump, my legs gave out and I rolled head over tail before turning into a puff ball and landing on my back. My arms and legs were flopped wide around me, my breathing was ragged, and my clothes were damp with sweat.

Vale scooped me up, cradling me in his arms against his chest while failing to hold back his laughter.

"Very dramatic, my love." Khade smirked at me as he picked grass from my hair. "Your somersault gave me an idea for next time, though, and I think you did well enough to add a third and fourth form too."

A hot bath and a warm meal later, we were lounging around when Shea and Tunder came through the portal and into the living room. Khade must have been expecting them because not only did he have nothing snarky to say about them coming in unannounced, but he stood and held out his hand in wait of something.

"Did you pull anything from them?" he asked when he had the two items in his hand.

"Nothing we can trace," Shea said as he sat down next to me, then nodded at Tunder, who was pouring himself a drink. "But they are from different senders."

Khade nodded and came over to hand me the two items. One was a plain envelope, and the other was high quality but with a broken wax seal. "What are these?" I looked at each of my brothers before staring up at Khade in question.

"As you know, we've been receiving anonymous tips from an unknown informant inside the NNC," he said as he went over to the drink cart and refilled his own glass. "Up until recently, we've operated under the idea that it's one person. Now, we believe there are two."

"Two informants?" My voice was high with the question. I was surprised, no doubt, but I was more excited about the possibilities this could provide.

"Axel and someone else?" Vale sat forward and took one of the envelopes from me.

"Axel's potential involvement hasn't been confirmed," Khade was quick to add.

"Or denied," Vale refuted.

"Regardless, there is a second informant. That much has been confirmed," Tunder spoke up, cutting off the potential argument.

"This is what you were called earlier for?" Khade nodded in answer to my question. "How did you confirm they were from different people?"

"When we first started getting secret missives, they were addressed to you and have continued to be addressed to you and your knights since," Shea said. "They've also been like that one—invitations to parties, minor information updates about the group, and some warnings we've been able to act on."

"And the other?" I asked, pulling out the papers from the plain envelope when a loose business card fell out that read *Azael Stonebrook, Spring Court Councilman.*

"Those were addressed to me," Khade said, and Vale and I both looked up at him. He continued before either of us could say anything. "We don't know why. Not yet. But those were addressed to 'the queen's council' with my name under the title."

I accepted his answer and looked down at the business card again before handing it off to Vale. "Nothing subtle about that."

I unfolded the rest of the papers. The first was a flyer with the slogan Step into the *New Night: Reclaim Your Freedom!,* but it was different from others I'd seen. It was formatted to look like a school flyer, complete with the Valley Hill Academy crest and The Wasp mascot.

"Why does it look like this?" I was annoyed that the school and logo were being used as propaganda.

"Those are new. They are personalizing them to each realm, school, and town now. Our PR advisors say it's meant to instill familiarity and trust, hoping to gain support," Tunder answered me.

"It should be illegal," I grumbled and looked over the other pieces of paper. "What..." My eyes flicked back over the three articles—three obituaries. "What is this?" My eyes swam. The papers felt heavy in my hands, and though I didn't know who these people were, I felt their loss as a sudden and intense wave of sadness filled my chest. "Who are they?" I asked, my voice barely above a whisper.

"We don't know who those two are yet." Shea pointed at the top two pages. "And we have no idea what it means, or why we were sent them, but we're looking into it—into who they were."

Vale had been looking at them next to me when he moved his hand from my thigh. "May I?" He held out his hand in ask of the papers.

I traded him for the thicker envelope that he had yet to open. Inside was a beautiful invitation. The softly deckle-edged parchment was cream and delicately bordered with gold foil. At its crown, a wreath monogram of pressed flowers encircled the letter S, and below, a graceful script written in shimmering gold added an air of elegance.

"'You are cordially invited to The Unity Soirée, an evening dedicated to the celebration of a special union. Join us for a night of joy and festivity as we make a momentous announcement,'" I read the words aloud but skipped the location, certain I knew who the host was. Still, I glanced at Vale for confirmation. "Is this Azael's address?"

He nodded, taking the invitation from me to look it over. "Is there any more information about this party?" He looked at my brothers, then at Khade.

"Just what you have there." Khade tipped his head at the invitation.

"We could only confirm that flowers, food, and champagne were ordered and scheduled for delivery to Azael's home on that date. Nothing more," Tunder added.

"So it could mean anything," Vale huffed as he handed me the invitation and went back to reading the obituaries.

"Or nothing." Shea sipped his drink. "He's thrown more parties in the last three months than both Queens combined."

"What's a unity soiree?" I asked, looking at the invitation again.

"Unity has been used in the propaganda. So it's likely something to do with the movement but written vaguely or in some code we haven't cracked yet." Tunder shrugged. "All the party invitations we've received look the same."

"So why do you think these are two different senders, then?" I didn't understand how they investigated these things or came to the conclusions they did.

"The timing, for one," Khade said. "We've never received two pieces of information at the same time. It's not impossible that the sender could have sent both, but unlikely based on what we've patterned of what we've previously received."

"Which is the second reason we suspect it's a different person." Shea reached over and took one of the papers from Vale. "Everything up to this point has been strictly information that we can lead back to Azael or his followers in one way or another. Parties, meetings, power moves, etc. Nothing as far off as obituaries."

"And if we assume Axel has been the one sending information up to this point, it's safe to say he didn't send the second. Two of those people died decades before he was born. They have no known connection to him, Azael, or anyone affiliated with the NNC," Tunder said.

"So far as we know," Khade added. "It's still under investigation. Old mail is being reviewed in case something was missed. But given that this information came with Azael's business card, along with a flyer from Valley Hill, and the movement originated in the Spring Court, we can presume a connection."

"And this third obituary," Vale said, lifting and waving it like the red flag that it was.

"Yes," Khade confirmed, and my brothers agreed.

"Why? Who's the third person?" I took the paper to look at the picture of the man.

"It's Axel's mom's other mate. He was killed in an accident shortly after Axel was born."

Chapter Seventeen

Another week passed at the cabin, and while I relished the uninterrupted time with my mates, my unrestricted ability to practice my magic and shifting, and the peaceful surroundings, I couldn't deny that I was growing increasingly stir-crazy. Portalling back and forth to the castle wasn't enough liberty after getting the taste of the freedom I'd experienced living on campus.

I argued that I was glamoured and didn't understand why I couldn't at least visit my friends or have dinner in public, but it was being in public that everyone was worried about. That I could accidentally be caught up in something again was the concern, not my identity exposure. The violence had steadily increased after Khade's press conference as protesters turned demonstrators, so I had been strictly forbidden until it settled down and a provisional security detail was put into place.

Not to mention the new but unsolved lead that one of our anonymous informants had left us. It was still unclear what the connection to Azael or the NNC had to the other two obituaries. They both had died so long ago it didn't make sense. Their families had been cleared of any connection to known associates of the NNC, and most importantly, Azael, who was the presumed leader. The man and woman were a newly mated couple, commoners who'd lived in the Spring Court. Her name was Unnai, his was Ceallach. She was a primary school teacher, and he was an ice technician at the ports. Their deaths were unusual but not unheard of. He died of exposure while doing routine ice removal, and she was accidentally poisoned while foraging with her students in the woods.

There was nothing more, leaving us and the reason for the tip shrouded in mystery.

Why they came with Azael's bond mate's obituary was also unclear. Aside from the peculiarity of his death, it didn't make sense either. Cyril Stonebrook was an environmental geologist testing new energy programs and was on a work trip when he fell from a cliff. His affinities were water and fire, and his shifted form was a leopard, so he couldn't save himself. There were others around, but not close enough to help in time. It was investigated and reported that an unusual but small seismic event had happened around the same time. However, as far as they could tell, he'd wandered too close to the edge and simply slipped off.

Knowing what we knew now, was it a consideration that Azael or someone close to him under orders had committed murder? Yes. But with no evidence or further clues, it ended the same as with Unnai and Ceallach—nowhere.

Khade and I had just returned from dinner with my parents when Vale came bustling down the hall, dropped his gym bag with a clunk, and swept me up in his arms to pepper kisses all over my face.

"What is all this about?" I giggled, wrapping myself around him.

"I'm making your dreams come true." He beamed at me.

"You've already done that." I blushed, though I don't think he saw the stain on my cheeks because as soon as the words were out of my mouth, he growled and crushed his lips to mine for a searing kiss.

When he pulled away, I was breathless and aching where he was between my legs. "And I'll keep doing it forever, my sweet mate." He kissed my nose and each of my cheeks while palming my ass before he straightened to look at Khade. "I did what you wanted."

"And what might that be?" Khade didn't look up from the pile of paperwork he was flipping through. He simply lifted his bourbon for a sip and kept reading while waiting for Vale's answer.

"Axel told me he'd be my informant."

Khade's head snapped up so fast the movement made the liquid in his glass slosh out.

I was surprised too and involuntarily tensed at the announcement. "How..."

Vale's features softened when he looked at me before setting me down. "Honestly, it didn't take much. I ran into him last week as I was going to training. He asked what I was doing, why I was doing it, and why you weren't back at school. So I told him, and today he came to me and said that he'd do it."

"He'd do what exactly?" Khade cocked his head and squinted at Vale. "What did you tell him, Vale?"

"I told him that her parents only agreed to allow her back on campus after the Night Guard's presence was made permanent, but that if those responsible weren't found soon or there was another attack, that they'd pull her indefinitely. Which was why I joined, so I could protect her and infiltrate the NNC myself."

"Why—"

"You did what?!" Khade slammed his glass down and yelled.

"I figured we'd get an answer where he stood one of two ways. Either he'd go to his dad and tell the NNC that I wanted to spy on them, or he'd help me instead. I was right. He joined the guard a couple of days ago, and today after practice, he told me he'd help me with my project."

"That's not enough," Khade snapped. "It could be a ruse to feed you false information."

"Agreed, which is exactly what Axel said when he handed me this file." Vale reached into his bag and pulled out a folder. "He said, and I quote, 'I don't know how else to convince you and I can't make up for what's been done, but I'll never stop trying. Give this to your new friend.' I was confused at first, but considering what we were talking about, I guessed he meant Puck, and based on the list of names, pictures, and the other documents in there, it's a folder full of proof."

Khade took the packet from him, and the more he flipped through the pages, the tighter his jaw clenched, but there was also a resolute gleam in his eyes.

"Many of the names are people we've already had suspicions about. Some are new, though, and that's significant. The travel dates and code names correspond with our intel. We'll need to verify the financial records and the rest of the details, but if this checks out..." He looked at Vale. "We'll need more evidence, but if everything can be confirmed and if he wants to earn any kind of redemption for whatever part he's played willingly or otherwise, this is a promising start. I'll also need to speak to him personally. If this is a ploy, he won't be able to lie to me."

"Which was something else he hinted at in a convoluted way," Vale added.

"How so?"

"It was weird, and it took me a bit to understand what he was getting at." Vale shook his head as if the conversation still confused him. "But it's how I knew he meant for me to give the file to Puck. He said he didn't understand how I could be friends with someone who scrutinized everything that came out of my mouth. I had no idea what he meant, but he kept bringing it up. Finally, I asked him what the hell he was talking about, and he said, 'Doesn't he have truthsayer?' We went back and forth again until I told him he was thinking of you, which isn't a secret—the entire realm knows of your abilities." He held up his hand to my winter mate when Khade's eyes narrowed. "Then he goes, 'So Puck really was just good at Starball and not using his ability to win? That's good to know. I didn't like the idea of him using it on me.' He stared me in the eyes when he said this, then tapped the folder again and said, 'My mental barriers aren't good enough to hide anything from a truthsayer.'"

"He knows Puck has access to you." I looked at Khade. "Axel may be a lot of things, but stupid isn't one of them."

Khade stared at me for a few beats before nodding. "If he's under a geas, he would need to find creative ways to ask for help and give information."

Acknowledging for the first time that Axel could be under the control of magic was a big step. We'd all tiptoed around it, volleyed ideas about the ways Axel could be under someone's command. Vale and I were strong proponents for it, my parents to a lesser degree, while my brothers were reluctant and would oscillate in their opinions. But if there was one unwavering holdout, it was Khade.

I was spinning all this in my mind, the conversations we'd had, the squabbles, the agree-to-disagree truces, all while he held my eyes before coming to stand in front of me.

"Axel asking to speak to me in a reticent way, knowing my magical capabilities, isn't something to balk at," he told me sincerely. "We need to consider everything and use all resources, and everyone willing and able at our disposal." He lifted his hand and ran the back of his knuckles down my jaw, watching me with his eyes as he spoke. "I won't ever forget what's been done to you, and I'll be hard-pressed to forgive anyone who's hurt you, voluntarily or not, and I will do everything in my power to make those responsible pay." His eyes darkened for a moment, his pupils turning to slits before he bent closer to me. "But for you, I will be open-minded and understanding."

Chapter Eighteen

I'd only been off campus for a few weeks, but walking through the quad felt different. Students and staff busied themselves coming and going from buildings and classes. The lawn, trees, and flowers had all been repaired or regrown. There was no evidence of vandalism or scorch marks from the fire, and the statue of the first queen had been righted. Still, it felt blotted. The invisible scars the NNC's attack had left behind dimmed the once lively academy. Even with the repairs made, they'd taken something from us, and it wasn't just the assumed safety but the joyful innocence that everything was right with the realms. The visible guards were an additional reminder—welcomed, yes, but a clear and obvious sign that things had changed.

There was still conversation and laughter, but it lacked a level of carefreeness I'd become accustomed to. Even with Callie by my side, I couldn't shake the little bout of despair I felt.

"I told you; it's sad here now," Callie whispered to me. She'd warned me that everything felt different, but I couldn't fully grasp what she'd meant until now. "Everyone's jumpy and constantly looking over their shoulder."

She was right. As I observed the student body, their eyes constantly flicked around, almost expectantly, while they kept their arms and belongings close, like victims ill at ease in their home after a robbery.

"Hopefully, that will change and everything will go back to normal soon." I gave her a small smile, though it felt as forced on my face as the ones I'd seen on everyone else's. "The security has been improved, and the guards are here now. There shouldn't be any more problems."

"Maybe." She ripped a flyer off the wall and held it out so both of us could read it. "But this kind of crap doesn't help," she sneered.

I agreed, but I kept my mouth shut. It was a standard-size piece of paper with nothing more than a slogan printed over a raised fist. *Dawn of a New Night: Unleash Your True Power. Join the Coalition Today!* it read.

There were more, each with a slightly different message

Join The New Order, Embrace the New Night!

Rise with the New Night: Find Your Strength!

Burn Bright, Rise Strong: Unite with the New Night!

The last one left a bad taste in my mouth, given its potential connection to the fires that'd been spread.

I wanted to do the same as Callie—rip the flyers down and burn them to ash—but as unfortunate as it was, they had the right to spread their message since it was rooted in equality. Without proof to the contrary, any action taken by the crown could be seen as an attempt to suppress dissent and an infringement on free speech.

I would do nothing to stop Callie or anyone else who wanted to rid the school of the message, though, and each time she caught my eye, I gave her the tiniest smirk in solidarity.

"I'm going to put together a clean-up crew," she announced loudly. "First order of business: throw away the litter!" she hollered and made a big show of tearing up the pamphlets and dumping them in the trash.

Some students cheered her on and took down the ones nearest them, while others, who were too far away or didn't have one within their sights, cheered or clapped. But the few who kept quiet or gave her a dirty look made my stomach clench. Out of the thirty to forty students around, there were only about two or three who didn't look impressed with her rant. If that number tracked through the entire school, for every one hundred students, that would be around three percent.

Three percent was a lot when it had been zero only a few weeks ago.

Jed was waiting for Callie when we rounded the corner, and the smile he gave her warmed my troubled heart. It was the first genuine one I'd seen all day, and even though it wasn't for me, I basked in it anyway.

"Have I told you how happy I am for you?" I tapped her with my elbow as she looked at him with a blush. She'd always had that special look on her face when she saw him, but now that they had found their mate group, it meant so much more.

"Not since the last time." She bumped me with her shoulder.

"Hey, Jed."

"Hey, Lyra." He pulled Callie from me and tucked her under his arm. "Glad you're back. Maybe my bunny will stop pouting now."

Callie wrinkled her nose, scowling at him. "I haven't been pouting."

"Sure you have." He booped her, then swooped down and kissed her before she could rant at him.

My cheeks hurt from smiling. They were so freaking adorable. "I missed you guys," I gushed. "I'm so happy for you."

"How many times has she said that today?" Jed mock-whispered in her ear while looking at me.

"Eight. But twice in the last two minutes."

"Ooh, a new record."

They jested at my expense, but I couldn't even be peeved because I was genuinely happy for them, and this was also totally adorable.

Callie rolled her eyes at me like she knew exactly what I was thinking. "Ugh, let's go before you combust into heart-shaped butterflies or something," she snickered, taking my hand with her free one and pulling me alongside them.

"I'm just—"

"I know," she cut me off with a giggle. "Geesh, you're such a sap."

"Are you excited?" Jed asked me over the top of Callie's curls. If she'd been wearing a ponytail, like she tended to do while working, he wouldn't have been able to see me, but today her hair was in an intricate lace braid that held her locks, leaving only a long woven tail to rest over her shoulder.

"I'm impressed, more than anything. Curious, though a bit nervous, but I trust you two." I picked up Callie's braid and looked it over. I knew she couldn't do this to her own hair. "Who did this?"

Callie's cheeks pinked, but she ignored me and pushed open the door to their lab. "Oh look, we're here! What a bummer I can't answer any more of your questions!" she hollered as she bustled into the room, flipping on lights, dumping her bag on a chair, and grabbing this or that while loudly humming to herself.

"You'll tell me, eventually," I grumbled at her, taking my usual seat while Jed locked the door and put up a privacy spell.

When she knew it was safe, Callie rolled out a buzzing box while Jed scrubbed his hands and brought over the tray she'd assembled. It seemed very practiced in their coordination, but they'd always worked well around each other, knowing what was needed. What one wouldn't do, the other did without question. A balanced lead to the others follow. It was so obvious that they belonged together.

Callie's hands landed on each side of my cheeks before she turned my face to look her in the eyes. "Did you hear anything I just said?"

"You didn't say anything." I raised a brow at her.

"But if I had, you wouldn't have heard it since you're in dreamy la-la land. This is important."

I nodded, or tried to, in between her hands. "I'm listening. You have my full attention."

She dipped her chin once, then released me to pull off the cover of the box.

I was a little speechless. I hadn't seen anything like what I was looking at before, even if part of me wanted to recoil. "They're beautiful." I moved closer, bending to crouch down to get a closer look before jerking back up and taking a step back. "They're safe, right?"

Callie rolled her eyes again. "Of course! I would never put you in danger. They're why we are here."

"And what are they exactly?" I asked, aiming to take a closer look at her reassurance.

Jed came over and put his hand on the box. "These are nullibuzzers," he announced with a big grin.

Callie put her hands on her hips. "No, they're not. We're not calling them that! They're nulliflies." She beamed.

"How is that any better than nullibuzzers?" Jed argued.

Callie shrugged. "It's cuter. Like a butterfly, except for a bee."

"But they're not bees, are they?" I asked. I mean, they looked like bees, sort of, but they weren't bees or I'd be getting warning signals while they scrambled to get as far away from me as possible. Plus, they weren't yellow and black.

"They are anti-bees," Jed said, opening the lid to coax one of the big fluffy blue and white nulliflies onto his finger. "They are the exact opposite of a traditional bee. Think of them as half-siblings or cousins of twins."

"And how exactly did you come up with this idea? Now that I'm looking at them, maybe I'll understand better." I kept my distance from the one Jed was holding and went back to examining the hive of blue and white not-bees tucked safely behind the glass.

Callie had explained to me several times what they were working on during the last couple of weeks, but I wasn't qualified to understand this level of biogenetics. Plus, seeing and believing were two different things.

"After we explained what we were working on to our mates, they offered to help, and together we created these." Callie bent next to me. "We told them we were trying to find a cure, and Jed made an offhanded remark about breeding a bug with anti-venom. The idea probably came because his mind is always in the gutter, and I'm pretty sure he has a breeding kink," she babbled.

"Gross." I pinched my lips.

"She doesn't need to know that, babe." Jed put the nullifly back in the box all normal-like as if we weren't talking about things best left in the bedroom.

Callie batted her hand at him and continued, "Anyway, Atlas didn't take it as a joke and thought it was a great idea, and apparently Elle likes a challenge, so we began brainstorming. She's an ecological geneticist, so she genetically modified a queen bee by altering specific genes in its DNA. Instead of producing allergens, like native bees do in their venom and honey, the meta bees now produce enzymes that neutralize those allergens."

"We tested your blood and skin cell samples multiple times against the queen's venom and will do the same with the midnight nectar—that's what we're calling the honey—to ensure there weren't any adverse reactions," Jed explained.

Callie rolled up my sleeve and continued, "Atlas is conducting field trials on soil, water, plants, and other insects and organisms to ensure the nulliflies don't disrupt the ecosystem. And we tested the venom on ourselves and others who don't have the allergy to ensure it's safe for the general population too."

I nodded along, hearing the words but still not fully grasping what was being said.

"And you used your divination to mature them?" I guessed. Callie had adaptation alchemy and could enhance the growth cycles of living things on a small scale. She used it with her plants all the time, but I'd never seen her use it on something like this.

"Yep. I shama-lama-ding-donged the first couple of larvae the mutated queen had reproduced so we could start clinical trials. I'd only ever done it with caterpillars before, so I could only mature a few drones and a new queen. Once they hatched, the modified honeybee queen's reign was over, and this pretty girl took over and began reproducing these larvae. They should begin hatching in another week, and then we'll have more to work with."

I stared at the blue and white honeycomb, with the fluffy blue and white queen bee and her few drone helpers as they tended to the new breed.

"We'll test these samples of yours when they hatch. After we get medical clearance from your doctor, the next step will be controlled exposure treatments," she said, healing the little mark she'd made by taking my blood.

"You two are amazing."

"We know." Callie batted her eyelashes at me.

When they were finished, we left the lab, and after confirming our dinner plans, Jed pulled Callie into him. "See you tonight." He smirked as they turned together and continued down the corridor.

I was only a few steps away from my class when Axel's pacing form came into view. Before I knew what I was doing, I rushed up to him and threw my arms around him, pulling him into a hug.

Chapter Nineteen

"Lyra?" He stiffened for a second before relaxing and returning the gesture.

I was grateful to him. I couldn't tell him that, but I was. He was helping us, and because of him, we would have an advantage over the NNC we hadn't before, which meant that the kingdom and everyone I loved would be safe again soon. All the information he'd given to Vale had checked out, and he'd passed Khade's interrogation with flying colors. Plus, since he was now officially a spy for the crown, he'd been placed on the same guard team training with Vale, making him part of the inner circle, even if unknowingly.

"Hi, how are you?" I beamed up at him.

He scanned my face, looking bewildered as he glanced around as if expecting someone to jump out and laugh at him. "I'm fine... How are you?"

"Really good." I stepped back to give us some space. "I never got the chance to thank you for saving me again. Thank you, Axel."

His shoulders relaxed, and his features softened. "You don't have to thank me, Lyra. My instinct will always be to protect..." He let the words drift off before clearing his throat and continuing. "I'm glad I was there and that you're okay. It's nice to have you back."

"Yeah, thankfully my parents finally relaxed enough to let me." I laughed it off. "With Vale doing guard training and all the extra security, they finally gave in. They were probably just getting tired of me always bugging them." I chuckled.

It wasn't even a lie since I had been pestering my parents so much. I knew they were exasperated with me, and I was positive that if Khade didn't like me so much, he would have thought me a brat too. Maybe I was a brat, but his punishments for it were nice.

"I doubt anyone would ever tire of you." He looked away and shoved his hand in his pocket. He'd said it so quietly; I didn't think it was meant for a response, and since it was another of those subtle flirts he would say to me sometimes, I wasn't sure how to take them. So I changed the subject like a pro.

"You look better than the last time I saw you."

Axel snapped his eyes back to mine, and I held my breath. I hadn't meant for it to be an insult.

"I've been sleeping more." His voice was low, and his focus intent. "My dreams have been ... interesting. So much so, I've been chasing them."

"Oh?" My voice cracked as my palms sweated.

"One in particular, actually."

I bobbed my head up and down like an idiot and turned away. "Well, I'm glad you're sleeping better." I adjusted my bag as I moved toward our classroom. "We should..." I nodded toward the door.

"Yeah." His voice was light, and if eyes could smile, his were at me.

I hoped he was laughing at my awkwardness and not because I'd inadvertently admitted to dream-walking into his private space. I wasn't positive that he'd seen me on his bed that night—the incident had happened so fast—but if he had, I definitely didn't want him reading anything more into it than an accidental power slip.

The classroom was loud with conversation, but I could feel Axel's eyes on me as we made our way to our assigned table, so I couldn't concentrate on anything but keeping myself upright. Once I was safely seated and no longer in danger of tripping over my feet and looking like a fool, I busied myself and tried to eavesdrop on the conversations around me instead of dwelling on if he'd seen me as a naked apparition in his bed or not.

There was some talk about the NNC and the fliers, but most of the chatter centered around the guards who patrolled the campus. One table talked about how they didn't think it was necessary for them to be here, which I heavily disagreed with. The rest of the groups seemed more interested in discussing the guards' physical attributes, the attention they were getting from them, and the dates they'd gone on.

"Axel," a female from the table behind ours whispered to him once he'd taken his seat.

He ignored her and continued to stare straight ahead, balancing his pen between his fingers.

"Dude, I know you can hear me," she complained, and when he didn't move or respond, she grumbled. "Ugh. You're such a dick."

Curiosity got the best of me, and when I turned to look at her, she perked up and smiled at me. "You're Lyra, right? I'm Dina. Will you ask him if his trainer has a mate?"

"Uh ... sure." I turned to look at Axel, who was looking at me. "Is your trainer single?"

He was fighting a smile, but he answered me with a shrug. "I think so."

"What's his name?" Dina followed up the answer with another question.

Axel remained silent as he kept his eyes on my face. I cocked my head and raised my brows. "What's his name?" I asked him, and he smirked at me.

"I don't know. He makes us call him captain."

"Will you ask him next time you go to drill?" Dina asked him while looking at me.

It was an odd conversation.

"No." Axel shook his head, answering me after I'd relayed the question.

"Will you at least ask him if he's mated or dating?" She was getting annoyed now.

"No." He looked me over before turning his focus to the front of the class again.

"Come on, he's hot!"

"His dating life isn't any of my business," he said, sort of responding to her but not really, since he was still speaking when she cut him off after his initial no.

"You're so lame," she grumbled, then turned to another table to see if they knew anything about the person training them, which was a different guard than the one in charge of Vale and Axel's group.

"That was weird." I scrunched my brows. "Why wouldn't you talk to her?"

Axel seemed to pause for a moment before turning to look at me, his face open but serious. "Because, unless it's required, I have no intention of ever speaking to another woman in your presence again."

I was stunned into stillness.

What could I possibly say to that in this moment that would ever suffice for everything that needed to be asked or said about his statement?

We stared at each other in silence, unmoving—unblinking—while the clamor continued around us. His gaze was so heavy it seemed to root me in place. Still, the seconds ticked by as I was held captive by the depth of Axel's eyes until Professor Rootsworth called the class to attention.

When I finally looked away, it took me a moment to grasp what she was saying. I focused on her, repeating the words she was saying in my mind until she had my full attention, listening as she went over our updated class schedule. But the space between Axel and me remained charged, which only grew the more she told us about our new assignments.

Evidently, the hiatus after the attack and the study restrictions, including the suspension of field trips, had put us so far behind in our classwork that we would need to put in extra time beyond our regular workload. Beginning today, we needed to coordinate with our partners for extra practice sessions outside of class to make up for the missed assignments.

I barely had time to adjust to the idea of spending so much extra time with Axel before she was instructing us to gather our things. There was a lot of grumbling conversation—as we followed Professor Rootsworth down the hallways and through the quad—about the inconvenience this would be to people's lives and schedules. Thankfully, the majority of the ire was directed at the rebels who were responsible, not at the school or instructors for doing their jobs. All around me, phone calls were being made and text messages sent by my peers, canceling or rearranging plans as they begrudgingly adjusted their schedules.

"Do you need to make arrangements?" Axel asked, casually walking alongside me. The only reason it was awkward was because I knew we'd be touching soon.

"Nope." I shook my head. "I'm all good." I cleared my throat, then lowered my voice from the higher pitch I'd answered him with. "Do you?" Did my voice just squeak?

Axel's lips twitched in my peripheral. "Nothing important. I'll take care of it later."

I nodded and adjusted my bag for the third time, then focused ahead of me and pretended not to notice each time he flicked his eyes at me to stare.

It was about a ten-minute walk following the professor, who led us to a clearing in the forest surrounding the school. The space was larger than the Starball field and encircled by tall trees, but with the midday sun, it was bright. We dropped our belongings near the edge and followed her into the middle, where she wasted no time giving us further instructions.

"In light of recent events, we will be incorporating a practical blend of both offensive and defensive magical principles in today's assignment. Our focus for this exercise is elemental oscillation—a skill that involves creating both an earth shield and a quicksand trap. This unique project aims to enhance your proficiency in smoothly transitioning your earth powers between solid and liquid states, fostering adaptability and control, all within the context of collaborative teamwork." She explained what she meant as she demonstrated her expectations before assigning us a location. "You have two hours," she said before creating a chair and side table from stone to sit back and observe her class.

"This should be a breeze for you," I told him as we walked side by side to our designated spot. He'd already proven that he could create an earthen shield when he protected us from the blast and then lifted the tree from Professor Farellaw.

"Don't sell yourself short, sunshine. I've seen you practice sifting."

"When?" I chose to ignore the nickname and instead focused on the rest of what he'd said. "Are you spying on me?" I quipped, knowing he wouldn't tell me if he was but curious how he'd react to the suggestion.

He looked away. "We share rejuvenation class together, and you and Callie can be loud." He smirked, then held his hands up in defense. "Not that I'm complaining."

My mouth fell open in mock horror. It was true. We got a bit giggly when we practiced magic. "We're loud?"

His smile grew as his eyes roamed my face. "Not in an obnoxious way. I like it. You have a nice laugh."

Turning, I focused on what the others were doing before suggesting we get started.

My first attempt was an epic failure. I pulled at the earth, gathering the dirt in a straight column like a wall, but when I released my magic, it crumbled into a pile.

"Well, I obviously don't know what I'm doing." I scowled at the dirt like it was at fault. "How do you do it?" I asked Axel, who was admiring my mess.

"My first suggestion would be to make it sturdier," he instructed without teasing me. "You need to have a solid foundation to build on, and a one-inch anything isn't going to stand on its own." He demonstrated what he meant, creating a thicker version of what I'd attempted. "There's more surface area to this, so it won't topple as easily."

Nodding, I tried again. I kept it closer to the ground and made it wider like his, and while it didn't completely give out when I released my magic, it didn't stay sound either.

"What are you using to stabilize it?" He knelt down to look at my mess.

"Stabilize what? I'm stacking dirt."

He took his hand and, without any force, easily swiped his fingers through the formation. "You're missing a binder to hold it together. The dirt needs support for the structure to hold. Like how rebar reinforces a poured plaster wall."

He looked up at me expectantly while I stared down at him like he was speaking in riddles. Which he was, because I hadn't known that.

"I know we don't know each other that well, Axel, but it might surprise you to learn that I've never poured concrete before. Or built a wall, for that matter. I don't even know what rhubarb is."

"Rebar, not rhubarb, which is a fruit." He smirked. "And it's steel, which acts as a backbone to provide the structure support."

"You can make steel?" My brows lifted, but he began shaking his head before I could question him more.

"I haven't tried, but I don't think so." He stood. "I just mean you need to reinforce the dirt with something. I piece the silt together like a puzzle and use my fire to heat the spaces between them, which acts as a glue to hold them together. Like brick and grout. The dirt is the brick, my fire is the grout, and the structure is sturdy to build on. Does that make sense?"

My shoulders relaxed at the explanation. "Yes, very much."

"Can I show you, like I did with the sifting?" He held out his hand.

I didn't hesitate, slipping my hand into his, first feeling the heat of his skin before the contact, watching intently as his fingers closed around mine, bringing our palms closer together. His hand wasn't rough or soft like mine, but solid and hardy instead of delicate. When he pulled at me to step closer, I went willingly, and when he moved behind me to wrap his arms around me, I had to concentrate on what we were doing when all I could really think about was leaning into him.

When his magic nudged at me, my pulse quickened and my core twitched.

"Let me in." His voice was low next to my ear, and my mouth parted at the thought.

When I dropped my barriers and our magics mingled, we both tensed at the onslaught. Axel guided our hands together over the dirt, intensifying his as he demonstrated the technique. I could feel as the tiny grains settled into place, sparking for a nanosecond before welding together. Piece by piece, he stacked them until the sum became a whole, shaping them into the bricks he'd described, then turning them into a short wall. It should have been overwhelmingly complicated, but the intention of what he wanted flowed through his elements to produce what he desired.

He repeated the exercise with different shapes and sizes, creating walls with flat profiles like plaster or with designs like a lattice, changing the technique slightly to highlight the differences in the build, where to provide support and strength, and how to shape and size them.

It was enlightening. To learn magic this way was a gift, and I was amazed by him.

When it was my turn, I tried to replicate what he'd done, but he was so adept in the skill that my work wasn't even close to what he'd achieved. But the lessons helped, and by the time class was over, I wasn't grumbling over crumbled piles of dirt in frustration but excited about the janky knee-high stone wall I'd made.

"You should practice your fire," Axel encouraged as we walked behind the others in our group. "Vale's imperium talent is fire, and I know for certain he'd help you. He gave me a few pointers when I was struggling."

"I'll ask him tomorrow," I agreed through a stifled yawn.

When we were back on the quad, Professor Rootsworth casually dismissed us by hollering over her shoulder as she walked away. "Thanks for today."

"I'll walk you," Axel said, lifting his hand toward my dorm.

"That's not necessary." I tried to brush it off, but he just shook his head and started moving with me.

"I'd like to, Lyra, but I also told Vale I would, and I'd prefer to keep your dragon mate in my good graces now that we train together." He smirked.

I was too tired to argue, and even though it felt like I was being treated like a fragile egg passed between two spoons, I couldn't deny the pleasure I felt at being protected.

We only made it halfway to my dorm when Vale met up with us and took over as escort. I thanked Axel again after Vale and he exchanged pleasantries, then we went our separate ways.

"Can I keep you to myself for a while longer, or do you want to call it a night?" Vale asked, pulling me into him as we walked.

"You can steal me away anytime you wish." I smiled up at him.

He swooped me up into his arms, released his wings, and flew us over our balcony, where I left my bag before he took us into the air. The sun was just beginning to set, and I could feel the night moving in.

Welcoming the darkness, my magical strength replenished quickly, and though I was still tired from the long day, I no longer felt depleted.

"Where are we going?" I snuggled into him as I drifted my hand on the current, enjoying the wind as it slipped through my fingers.

"I found a place I want to show you," he said, tightening his hold around me. "I think you'll like it." He smiled like he was really pleased with himself.

He should be because it was perfect.

We arrived just as the sun was casting its final rays over the top of the summit, highlighting the glow from the flowing lava and turning the snow orange. Vale circled the peak and flew us down to a mountain glade, where the view was clear enough to see the rising moon and setting sun. It was a magical oasis that seemed to hold onto all the changing seasons while springing new life. On one side of the plateau, trees with autumn leaves nestled against those bearing fruit, while on the other were the buds of aconite peeking up through a dusting of snow near winter bushes of heath.

The snow-topped peak fed the cascading waterfall, sprinkling the grass, while the lava pool from the crater vent spilled down the opposite side, heating the air. In the center of the meadow, a large blanket was laid out, with a basket anchoring the top to hold it down.

As soon as my feet touched the ground, I could feel each of the elements surrounding us, communing together in perfect harmony.

"This is beautiful," I told Vale in awe, running my hands through the settled snow that sat on the rocks before picking an apple from one of the trees. It smelled like dry leaves, was cold like winter, ripe with summer, and sweet as spring. "Mmm," I hummed as I chewed and took the fruit to Vale to let him taste.

He took half in one bite, which made me giggle at him.

"These are my new favorite apples."

"Then we have plenty of reason to come back for more." He kissed me before bending to unload food from the basket.

"You packed a picnic?" I sank to my knees next to him, watching with hungry eyes to see what he'd brought.

"I thought you'd be hungry." He held out a bite of cheese for me.

"You were right. I'm starving." I took it and popped a grape in my mouth. Along with the cheese, there were crackers, fruit, nuts, spreads, sparkling wine, and water. He unwrapped an assortment of finger sandwiches, including tomato and cucumber, and teased me with huckleberry croissants stuffed with chocolate meant for dessert.

"This is perfect." I sighed happily, biting into an egg and chive sandwich.

"Just like you." He reached over to wipe mayo from my mouth.

We snacked as we watched the sun disappear over the horizon until it was dark enough for the stars to twinkle in the night sky. We talked about his classes, how his training was going, and he agreed to help me with my fire the next time we were at the cabin. After the wine was gone and the remaining food had been packed away and forgotten, I found I had enough energy to ride his cock under the full moon until we were both tired and fell asleep in each other's arms.

Chapter Twenty

"Hello, my mate." Vale grinned, running his fingers down the side of my face. "How was class?"

He knew exactly how my class had gone, and I was certain he still felt the rush of heat coursing through my body. Power sharing with Axel was becoming something of a problem for me and my hormones. Especially if it meant that Vale and Khade were feeling it too. Axel and I had spent nearly every day together for a week, catching up on our assignments. I didn't exactly have a choice since he was my partner, but I didn't know how much longer I could keep doing it. Each day, the lines got blurrier and confused everything further.

"Class was fine." I gnawed on my lip and tried to hide my blush by looking away and waving goodbye to the others.

"Just fine?" He blocked my view to whisper over my lips, making my aching center twitch with need.

The whimper that escaped me was involuntary. Vale's eyes widened at the sound, and in response, he wrapped his large hands around my face, tipped my head, and devoured my mouth as if we were alone in our dorm and not standing in front of Axel or a class full of students.

Fisting his shirt, I leaned into the kiss, pulling myself closer while pressing my thighs together in a fruitless attempt at some relief. I couldn't even enjoy that his teasing had backfired on him as arousal so potent pulsed between us and thickened the air. Vale released my face, wound one arm around my shoulders, and moved the other to first palm my ass before curling his fingers around to slip further between my legs. When he squeezed me, I jutted out my hips, pushing into his hand and moaned into his mouth.

"Fuck," Axel cursed quietly behind us, but it was mixed with a groan and heavy sigh before he cleared his throat. "Stop. Everyone's watching," he complained, moving closer behind me as if to block what Vale was doing from everyone's view.

Vale smiled against my lips before pulling back to stare down at me with heated eyes. "Let them look. Lyra's mine, and they should all know it." He tucked me under his arm and stood to his full height. "Or was there another reason you wanted me to stop?" Axel glared at Vale but didn't say anything in response, which in turn made Vale chuckle at him. "Too easy, man. Anyway, we were called to an impromptu training sesh."

Axel nodded down at me. "We should walk her home first."

"Lyra didn't tell you?" Vale poked him in the stomach.

Axel's brows lifted in question. "Tell me what?"

"She asked to watch next time we had training. That's why I'm here." Vale clicked his cheek at him and pulled me alongside him, keeping pace with me since his legs were so much longer than mine.

As we walked, he asked us how many more make-up classes we had, how it was going, and what he could do to help. I answered his questions, and Axel praised him for helping me with my fire element.

"She was able to build a dome today." He smiled at me.

"I think it's easier for me to stabilize the barrier with roots, though; I can do it faster, and it takes less energy and concentration."

Axel nodded. "We'll focus on that more next time, then."

"And we'll keep practicing with fire," Vale added. "Once you get it figured out, it won't tire you so much."

I grew eager when Vale and Axel switched the topic to their training. I was interested, but the closer we got to the location, the more animated Vale became, and it must have been flowing into me because I was excited too. I wondered how long I'd be allowed to stay and watch. I'd never seen a true training session before, and I was curious how it matched up to mine and how Khade and Vale had been training me.

When we arrived, I looked around expectantly. There were loads of guards, along with student trainees and staff, which was surprising. I didn't realize staff members were being trained too. But with them were court officials, which confused me. Then my breath caught when Khade's head snapped up and his eyes landed on me.

My pulse fluttered, and that same heat from before rushed through my body. If one of my mates didn't sneak me off somewhere and touch me soon, I was liable to explode on my own just from all the pent-up arousal coursing through me. My body was practically singing being so close to my mates.

"Sweet mate, I'll take care of you as soon as we get home," Vale whispered in my ear before flicking his tongue out against the lobe.

I doubt Khade heard Vale's teasing comment, but the way he adjusted his tie and visibly had to hold himself back, I knew he was feeling me and could probably guess what Vale had promised.

"Why are these people here?" I looked over to where a group of faculty members were.

"I don't know." Vale pulled me tighter against him. "It must be important for the Queen's Advisor to be here, though," he said.

I caught sight of Professor Warrock, and my heartbeat increased. He was standing with a group of guards, but I recognized him immediately, even with his back facing me.

"There's Irondale. We're with him, I'm assuming?" Axel said.

"Yeah." Vale squeezed my hip where it rested. "...quick, and then I'll get you home."

I didn't hear what he said as my breathing sped up, and I moved away from him. I knew what was happening now. Why I'd been excited and hot coming here. I'd been through it three times before, but it still surprised me—so much so I almost felt intoxicated.

Professor Warrock looked up at me when I was only a few feet away, and his eyes widened. He turned to face me fully, his lips tipping up into a broad smile, before he was jostled and promptly shifted aside. As soon as the dark male pushed himself through the group, his eyes locked on mine and the bond hummed in my chest. He was stocky, with rippling muscle from his thick neck to his corded calves, though his skin looked velvet to the touch. His pitch-black hair was cropped short and only slightly darker than his umber skin. Thick brows crowned his dark eyes that peered down at me past a wide nose. Burgundy lips parted as he took me in. When his eyes focused on mine again, a smile tugged at my lips, but as I moved faster toward him, he slowed his progress, and the minor faltering was enough to cause me to pause.

The slight hitch in his step ripped through me, stopping me in an instant. I brought my hands up to my chest as a tremor tried to take root between my breasts. The male's eyes narrowed as he took in my posture, but before I could process his actions further, he was in front of me.

"Mate." His voice was deep but gentle, a contradiction that seemed to mirror his impressive size. The tension between us was palpable, the silence stretching as he regarded me with an intensity that sent shivers down my spine. A thousand emotions flickered through those dark eyes, but one thing was clear—he was holding back.

Even as recently as a few weeks ago, his hesitation would have had me reeling in vulnerability, jumping to conclusions and assuming the worst. But I was stronger now, comfortable in my skin again, secure in the bonds I already shared, and confident in the ones to come. My matings were proving to be unusual, and I needed to be patient in the face of such surprises. Meeting your mate could happen at any time, but when it occurred outside of a revelry, the unexpected deserved a moment of grace.

Quiet seconds passed between us like hours in the sands of time. Then he took a measured breath as though he were steadying himself and took a small step forward. "Forgive my shock. I never expected this. Never thought I..." He let the words trail off as his eyes roved over my face.

He wasn't running or being cruel, but I felt vulnerable in the stillness. I just wasn't sure if it was his or mine. And in the end, my nerves got the best of me as tremors slowly wracked through my body.

"It's okay. You don't have to—" I made to step away from him to give him space so he could sort out what had just happened.

He reached out and wrapped his large hands around my arms to stop me from moving as his brows pulled down in earnest. "Whoa, hold on there, sugar. I may not deserve you, but you're mine and I'm not letting you go." He held me firmly, closing the distance between our bodies as he moved his hands up and down my arms as if to warm me. "What's your name?"

"Lyra." I tried to keep my voice from shaking, but it came out so quietly I was surprised he'd heard me at all.

"Lyra," he hummed and slid one of his hands up my neck to caress my face. "My name is Rhett, and though I may not be worthy of you, I trust in fate and I will try my very best to be deserving of you from this day forward. If you'll have me?"

My heart ached at his words, as I understood them all too well. I'd once believed I wasn't worthy too, but while my reasons were steeped in the sting of rejection, Rhett's were his own and a mystery to me for now. Hearing this, a simmering determination replaced my initial apprehension about this male. But I needed to be certain of his decision before I accepted him with mine.

"Are you sure?" I whispered.

"Oh, baby, I'm positive. This is the dream, and you are my fantasy come true. I want you. Unless I've already fucked this up?"

He peered down at me intently, though his eyes showed no fear—perhaps he was teasing. After all, who didn't accept their fated mate? Aside from his momentary hesitation, I could forgive him for being unprepared. We weren't at a revelry, and he hadn't expected to meet his mate on this random afternoon. He had been focused on instructing others in defense, not preparing himself for vulnerability.

"You haven't," I told him, determined to trust my magic and the gift of my fated bonds once more.

"Good. Will you accept me?" He lifted his hand and ran his calloused knuckles down my cheek. "Do you accept the bond?"

"Yes."

"Yeah?" He beamed down at me.

Smiling at his ambivalence, I agreed again. "Yes. Absolutely."

"Fuck yes." He pressed his full lips against me, working them open slowly before slipping his hot tongue into my mouth to tangle with mine.

When he hummed, I relaxed, and with my repose, he groaned as he deepened the kiss. Rhett's hold on me tightened, and when one heavy hand traveled down my back to squeeze my butt, I mewled into his mouth, which really set him off. He hummed again and pulled at my lips, nipping them before sweeping his tongue back inside against mine. When we finally pulled away from each other, my lips felt swollen, my cheeks were hot, and I was panting for breath.

"Fucking amazing." He swiped his thumb over my bottom lip, and the way his eyes flared and his hand stuttered on my skin, I wondered if he had the same thought as I did—him pushing his thumb between my lips for me to suck.

The tension between us ticked up a fraction, and with it, a small rush of warm wind blew my hair as it swept around us. It reminded me that we weren't alone, and when I looked around, I sucked in a breath at the shimmering privacy. We weren't completely secluded, but most of the guards and students had been blocked from view, and when my eyes landed on Vale, I knew he was responsible for the privacy. He winked at me and let the subtle heat waves he'd created with his magic dissipate.

Axel was beside him, inside the circle too, and the blank expression he gave us was one I didn't focus on for too long. It wasn't the time, and before the inevitable conversation happened with Axel, Rhett would need an explanation. Khade had moved closer too and was standing with Professor Warrock and the other staff, who looked at us with varying degrees of approval and interest. As the distorted heat waves disappeared, Vale approached Rhett and me, and with each step, his smile grew.

"Now you know why I was always so eager to get home," Vale snarked at Rhett and held out his hand.

Rhett chuckled at him, slapping their forearms together in a gesture.

"You're Irondale, his trainer?" I asked my new mate, though the answer was obvious in their greeting.

"That I am." He gave me a bright smile before looking back at Vale. "And had I known you were running off to my mate every night, I would have kept you longer and gone in your place." Rhett's deep voice vibrated through me where he held me to him.

Vale barked out a laugh. "No need. I like to share." He waggled his brows, and my cheeks flushed.

"Good to know." Rhett's voice lowered.

My stomach tightened at the insinuation, and my earlier frustrations reared up again. I could feel Khade's eyes on me, and even though he had to keep himself a secret until I revealed to Rhett, I already knew how he liked to share, and the thought had me nearly squirming where I stood.

"Does this mean training is canceled?" Vale bounced on the balls of his feet and rubbed his hands together. "'Cause I'm happy to skip class and take Lyra..."

"Unfortunately not." Rhett kept his eyes on me when he answered. "In fact, I'll be pushing you more than ever now that I know who you're protecting. I think I'll need to add private lessons to your regimen too." Vale's groan turned to intrigue when Rhett added, "For you and Lyra."

"What? No." Axel's voice was loud, almost angry at Rhett's statement, the assertion decisive enough that we all turned to look at him.

Vale snorted at his old friend, but Rhett cocked his head and responded slowly, his voice darkening dangerously.

"I didn't ask for your opinion, recruit." He said the last word almost like an insult. His features hardened into a mask of authority, and beside me, he seemed to grow taller and wider as he regarded Axel.

Axel ground his teeth and glared up at him, flicking his eyes at Vale, and then stared at me for a few seconds too long. Rhett's posture stiffened, and then he wasn't beside me but in front of me, blocking me from Axel's view.

"Do we have a fucking problem?" he sneered.

I couldn't see Axel anymore, but the ground beneath my feet rumbled with their exchange.

"No." Axel's voice was resonant and terse.

Vale moved around Rhett's wide body and pulled me against him with a smile. His warm, familiar comfort was enough for me to not worry about the interaction. Even if Rhett knew who Axel was, this wasn't something I would involve myself in. My mates needed to figure out their relationships with each other on their own and with little involvement from me. Not that Axel was my mate.

"You can't expect her to spar with you two," Axel spat.

Rhett stepped forward to stare down at Axel. "Who the hell do you think you are?"

"You could hurt her."

"I would never hurt my mate." Rhett shoved Axel, but Axel recovered quickly and was back in his face.

"She's too small..."

Rhett grabbed Axel's shirt collar in his fist and ground out between his teeth, "Mind your fucking business."

Axel glared back. "She is—"

"That's enough." Khade pushed them apart with very little effort. Or I should say, he pushed them apart by holding back Rhett and shoving Axel, who ended up stumbling to stay upright. Ignoring Axel's grumbling, Khade adjusted his suit jacket and tie and looked at Rhett. "You're on duty and causing a scene. Finish this on your own time." Then he gave me a quick once-over before focusing on Vale. "Take Ms. Bruadar home, then get back here. You three have work to do."

And with that, he turned and made his way back to the group he'd been conversing with, effectively ending the argument.

It was insanely hot, and I had to force myself to look away instead of watching him. Thankfully, Vale felt my struggle through our connection and swooped in to save me like the perfect mate he was. Stepping in front of me to block my view of Khade, he looked at Rhett. “I’ll be quick.”

“No. I’ll take her. You and the others will run laps while I’m gone.” Rhett nodded to the rest of the group, which now included Puck, Roko, Jed, Brev, and Sidric, whom I hadn’t seen or talked to since the winter revelry. They watched us, chatting among themselves, while Axel stood apart, staring us down. There were several others in the group that I didn’t know, but when Rhett whistled to get their attention, they all moved to stand in a line, waiting for his instruction. Without letting me go, he told them what he expected of them, and after he dismissed them, they all set off to run laps—all but Axel and Vale. Vale lingered only a moment to give me a quick kiss before turning to shove Axel into motion, who was still just staring at us with his arms crossed over his chest.

Rhett held Axel’s gaze and waited for them to turn and join the others before he looked down at me. “Is he an ex of yours, or am I misreading his reactions?” His deep voice vibrated against me where he held me to him.

Sticking as close to the truth as I could, I shook my head. “Axel and I have never dated. We’re partners in my elemental class, though. Vale knows him better than I do.”

Rhett looked up at them again, then hmphed to himself before taking my hand and turning us to walk away. “Was he interested and you turned him down? Is that why he’s mean-mugging me?”

I huffed out a single laugh and shook my head. “I don’t think Axel liked me very much until recently.” I didn’t want to talk about our past, simply because I wasn’t sure how to bring it up, especially knowing he worked so closely with Axel as his trainer. I wanted to consult with Khade and Vale first about how and when to best inform him. So, for now, I left it at that.

It was busy on the quad, with students either lingering or leaving campus to hit up the local bars since it was the weekend. We made casual conversation as we walked; I was curious about his job while he asked me what classes I was taking, all while ignoring the many women who greeted him or tried to get his attention.

Like Khade, Rhett had a bit of a reputation, one he'd earned over the last couple of weeks while being stationed here. It wasn't something I had paid much attention to, but it was hard to ignore now. I wasn't uncomfortable, and I couldn't blame the women. Rhett and I had only just met and been revealed as mates, and they couldn't possibly know that yet. And not everyone knew me or Vale to know that I was mated and would not be walking hand in hand with another male unless he was mine. For all they knew, I was just the lucky girl Rhett chose tonight and he was taking me back to his room.

To his credit, he didn't acknowledge them at all. He didn't look in their direction, didn't return their greetings, or even stop speaking to me if they tried to talk to him. We just continued toward the mated dorms, strolling hand in hand in conversation as if they weren't even there. It lined up with the bits of information I'd heard about his nightly activities. He didn't want conversation from them, and if they knocked on his door, he invited them in, got and gave what he wanted, and sent them on their way. Only one time did I hear someone complain, and all she'd said was that he didn't even ask her name. So with his undivided attention on me and with every insignificant question he asked, I was more and more comfortable with him, and soon, I was able to ignore them too.

Chapter Twenty-One

"There you are!" Callie rushed up to us from where she'd been pacing outside the mated dorm doors.

She and Jed had just moved in after renovating the space to suit their bond's needs.

"Jed texted me." She beamed, looking up at Rhett before jumping up and down and clapping her hands. "I'm so excited! This is amazing!" She squealed, then threw her arms around my shoulders.

After she was done gushing and squeezing the breath out of me, she pulled back and looked at Rhett again and introduced herself. "I'm Callie."

"Lyra's best friend. It's nice to meet you." He tipped his head in acknowledgment.

"You're a really big dude," she blurted out.

Rhett chuckled at her. "It comes with the territory. I work out a lot."

"But aren't you Sidhe Hounds just big anyway?" She tilted her head curiously.

"Yep. Just all part of the package." He rolled his shoulders with a drawl, almost as if gloating.

Callie literally didn't care and shrugged her shoulders before focusing on me again. "Do you want to hang out while they're running hills and doing pushups? My kitchen is freshly stocked with pizza and ice cream." She waggled her brows.

My stomach growled as if on cue, and Callie took that as a resounding yes to her invitation. Before she could run off and preheat the oven, I made plans with her for another time since it was already so late. She clasped her hands in front of her in triumph after holding me to a pinky promise, then gave Rhett a nod.

"It was nice to meet you. Welcome to the group." She gave him a cheesy smile before skipping off to her room.

"Callie and Jed are down that way." I pointed in the direction of their room when we were inside the main doors. "Their other mates work in the city but will probably be around often."

I explained how Jed and Callie were linked but not mated and had been involved for years, then pointed out Puck and Roko's dorm before I took him to ours. He looked around the living room but was more curious about the balcony and the forest behind the building.

"I scouted this unit and several others not long ago," he said, scanning the trees and exterior. "Now that I know the queen's son lives here, all these extra precautions make sense. I'm glad you're in this residence." He turned to me.

I was surprised to learn that he'd been the guard Khade had called in for the favor, and whatever look I had on my face he misunderstood, prompting him to explain further. "It was just a safety measure, likely due to all the trouble with the NNC. There's no indication that the Night duke is a target; it was more of an audit of the existing protections. The safety measures that were in place were already excellent; they're just better now. I didn't mean to alarm you." He came to stand in front of me, putting his large hands on my shoulders.

If I had been worried about my safety, his explanation and physical touch as if to anchor me would have reassured me. Instead, the relief I felt was because he wasn't questioning why Khade had asked him to do the recon, so he wasn't suspicious of the request.

This one little encounter made me eager for him to pass his tests so there weren't any more secrets between us. The more mates I found, the harder the geas was to hide behind, and I looked forward to the day that I didn't have to anymore.

"I'm just a little jumpy after everything that's happened," I told him.

"It's understandable. We're doing everything we can to ensure everyone's safety and find those responsible," he told me. "When I'm not training, I'm overseeing security patrols and working with operatives. We'll get these rebels nipped in the bud before you know it. Speaking of, I don't want to leave you, but I need to get back."

I nodded and walked him to the door. I wanted to spend time with him too. We'd just met, but I was meant to spend my life with him; I wanted to know him so we weren't strangers. After we exchanged numbers, I asked about his schedule. He was busy, and I wasn't sure when we'd be able to see each other again.

"Do you have a day off soon?" I asked hopefully.

"No." He shook his head, but before I could get lost in disappointment, he continued. "But I'm not waiting that long to see you again, doll. May I take you to breakfast tomorrow?" He laced his fingers with mine.

"I'd like that." I smiled up at him.

"Good." He released my hand to thread his fingers through my hair before bending forward to kiss me. He moved slowly as if to gauge me and allow me time to pull away if I wanted, but tilting my face up to meet his lips was as natural as if we'd been doing it forever, and my response was enough permission to encourage him.

Rhett's kisses were somehow hard and gentle at the same time, demanding yet exploratory, making me ache for more. His lips were fuller than mine, powerful, and sweet. He was warm, like an autumn evening when the air was humid with sultry heat as it simmered and held onto the last rays of the setting sun. Like the cascade glow from a radiant fire at twilight or the warmth that emanated from buildings and sidewalks, keeping the city balmy long into the night. Comfortable and cozy.

I could sense his restraint in the way he moved and held me to him. The careful way he kept his contact light as he gently moved against me, skimming me with his touch.

"You're holding back," I whispered against his lips.

"You're precious. I don't want to hurt you." His brown eyes were unsure, and his deep voice was filled with caution as his hot breath passed between us.

Wrapping my arms around his shoulders, I pulled myself closer to him. "You won't," I assured him. "Let me know you. Please."

Rhett's body stilled for a moment, his eyes searching mine as he regarded me. I didn't know yet what had given him pause, but I watched as his uncertainty turned to yearning. A low groan escaped on an exhale before he crushed his mouth onto mine.

Rhett was a boulder of a man. His hands were the size of my head, his arms and torso bulged with muscle, and one of his thighs equaled the size of both of mine.

He grabbed me around the waist, lifted me to him, spun, and pinned me to the wall. Holding me in place with his chest, he slid his hands down to pull apart my legs, anchoring himself between my thighs. The previous gentleness of his kiss had turned bruising instead as he did exactly what I'd asked of him—not hold back.

He squeezed my thighs, kneading my flesh with heavy hands as his tongue and lips consumed me. I mewled in his mouth at the taking, and when I pulled away to catch my breath, he moved his devouring mouth across my jaw and down my neck, nipping and flicking his tongue over me. The short stubble on his chin deliciously scraped against my soft skin, and the muscles around his shoulders rippled with his movement. His hair was cropped short, and the buzzed little hairs tickled my palms as I swept my hands over his head. As I scratched my nails over his scalp, he groaned before taking my mouth again.

If his phone hadn't interrupted us, I wasn't sure how far we would have taken things. Obviously, we wouldn't have solidified our bond—it was too soon for that—but that didn't mean there weren't other things to do in the meantime. The decision was made for us, though, when his ringtone echoed loudly in the quiet living room for the second time. He grumbled as he pulled away from me and yanked the cell out of his pocket, silencing the noise as if it had personally offended him.

When it was muted, he shoved it in his pocket again and wrapped his hand around my jaw to peck against my swollen lips. "I don't want to leave you."

Running my hands over his pecs, I returned his kisses. "We'll have more time tomorrow. Your job is important."

"Now more than ever." His deep voice vibrated between us as his dark gaze bore into me.

Once I was on my feet again and before we could even say our goodbyes, his phone was screeching from his pocket for the third time.

Rhett glared at the screen. "What?" he barked. "Yeah. I'm on my way. Don't call again." He hit the disconnect button, hanging up on the voice that was mid-response. "Sorry, doll, I've got to go. But I'll see you in the morning."

"Okay."

He kissed me once more and didn't leave until the door was closed and locked behind him. I waited and listened until the heavy thunk of his feet pounding down the hall had gone quiet. Then I kicked off my shoes and turned to go to my bedroom when a cool hand wrapped around my throat and pushed me up against the wall.

"I thought he'd never leave," Khade's low voice whispered over my lips before his tongue slipped between the seams.

All I could do was moan as he slipped his hand up under my shirt, gave my nipple a gentle pinch, followed by the pad of his thumb making tight circles over the hardened peak.

My shirt didn't stay on long, and when my bra was off and my breasts were free, he ducked his head to pull me into his mouth while he worked down my skirt.

I was still pent up from earlier and needy from my kiss with Rhett, so with Khade ravishing me, I was practically vibrating with desire.

"Khade." I whimpered when his finger teased over the lace above my clit, and a faint rattle emitted from his chest at the sound. When his eyes shifted into his Beithir form, a subtle purple glow cast between us as he sunk to his knees.

"You're soaked, little mate." His voice came out like a raspy purr, and even though I was hot, I shivered from his touch. He ran the tip of his nose between my legs, followed by his tongue over the gossamer silk. "I'm going to make this pussy feel so good." His hot breath wafted over my mound as his fingers slid between the fabric, running the back of his knuckles between my slit.

I nearly burst from his words and the simple touch of his hand. "Please."

Khade swept me up into his arms and kissed my swollen lips, but instead of the bedroom, he took us through the portals and back to the cabin.

"Why are we here?" I panted when he released my mouth.

"We can't have the Sidhe Hound scenting that I fucked you. Not until he reveals you to him."

He stood me on the bed, took my panties off, then instructed me to lie down. He held my eyes as he unbuttoned his shirt.

When Khade was undressed down to his boxers, his heavy gaze swept over me as he adjusted himself behind the silk he wore. "You're so beautiful, Lyra. Let me see what's mine."

My nipples tightened at his praise as I did what he'd asked and opened my legs for him.

Khade knelt near the edge of the bed and pushed me open wider as he lowered himself. "Who does this pretty pussy belong to?"

"You." I panted and tried not to squirm.

"Good girl." He hummed as he brought his mouth down onto me.

Clenching the bedsheets, I tried to hold myself steady, but Khade was a magician with his tongue, and my first orgasm ripped through me only moments after he sucked me into his mouth.

When my second orgasm rolled into a third and he still wasn't letting me up, I begged him for more. I was so sensitive from his intimate kiss, but I needed *him*.

"Please, please..."

"Give me one more, love," he whispered against my delicate flesh, then flicked his tongue over my clit as he pushed and curled his fingers inside me. "Come on my face again, pretty girl."

And I did as euphoric tears slipped from my eyes.

When he finally moved to kiss up my body, I collapsed against the bed, not realizing that I'd been holding myself tense from his attention. He laved me with sweet kisses, lavishing each breast with care, and when he reached my mouth, he pushed himself into me and swallowed my moan with a rhythmic murmur.

Wrapping one arm around my waist and fisting my hair with his other hand, Khade rolled himself into me hard and slow. His cock hit a spot deep inside that made my toes curl, followed by the perfect drag that seemed infinite because of his length.

I was so wrung out I could only hold on as he took what he wanted from me but giving me more in return.

"That's it; moan for me. Let go..." He slammed into me with a grunt as I did what he'd asked and cried out another orgasm. I was shaking, but he simply circled his hips as his breaths grew faster and heavy. "Yes. Again, Lyra."

"I can't," I whimpered, but even as I said the words, I could feel the pressure building as he worked himself against me. "Khade..."

Shifting himself, he pushed down on my hip as he tucked his legs up into a kneeling position, then he bound both of my hands in one of his against my stomach, wrapping the other around my throat to hold me in place. With just enough pressure, he squeezed the sides of my throat as he slammed himself into me.

"Look at me." He grunted. "That's a good girl. Now, give me one more. Come on my cock," he demanded.

I was shaking when something slipped over my clit. I tensed for a moment, unsure what was happening, but Khade's eyes shifted with a rattling groan, and that's when I knew.

"You feel so good. You're fucking perfect," he grit between his teeth as I writhed beneath him, bound by his hands and filled with his cock as his partially shifted tail tip quivered between us. As he continued to speak, I lost track of his words.

I was overstimulated, overwhelmed, and utterly at his mercy. My world shrank to our connection, where it was just him and me, existing in heightened pleasure as everything else faded away.

Watching him watch me only added to the experience, and as Khade's face contorted into pure bliss, a different swell of euphoria filled my chest.

I was unable to voice my happiness, but he could feel it through the bond, just as I could sense his joy.

After we bathed, I curled up against him to fall asleep on his chest and thanked the stars again for bringing him into my life.

Chapter Twenty-Two

Rhett

I cased the mated dorms once more before leaving. Just to make sure. Trusting people was hard enough with the work I did, but my mate was in there and after the bullshit with the NNC, my faith in the realm's citizens was practically nonexistent anymore.

As an operations specialist in the Night Guard, I'd overseen more security reports and arrests in the past year than in my previous three years in this position and six years as a guardsman combined. Thankfully, most of them were just pot stirrers—the same jackasses who started bar fights and graffitied anatomy on buildings late at night. Other joiners were those who'd always had a problem with authority, and if the NNC managed to take over the government, they'd turn on them eventually too. But the ones who believed the propaganda were alarming, and that was something the Crown and Citizen Advocacy Bureau would have to look into. That some felt so failed by the current system that they'd believe the rhetoric of a radical sect was disturbing. They were the ones who had me on edge the most. They'd already felt forgotten, and this mindset had led them to believe they had nothing left to lose, making their actions the biggest danger to society.

Thankfully, the spells that had been in place were even stronger now than when I'd first carried out my security check. Being grateful that the queen's son was my mate's neighbor was something I thought I'd never say. I respected her Majesty and the Knight Lords, but Puck was a brat, and nepotism pissed me off. Until now.

"Hello, captain," another female called out to me, waving her fingers and batting her eyes to draw my attention. Which she didn't get.

The rumor mill about me finding Lyra wasn't spreading fast enough for my liking. Ignoring them and hoping they'd catch a clue wouldn't work either, since engaging in conversation and getting to know the people I took to bed was never on the agenda. If they were brave enough to approach me for sex, I fucked them and sent them on their way—a page I'd taken from Khade's book after hearing his reasons why. I'd had a few friends with benefits over the years, and the only time that had ever become a problem was if they wanted more. I hadn't been interested then, and I certainly wasn't now. I'd have to somehow move along the spread of gossip.

I wondered if that brat, Puck, could be useful. He was friends with Vale. Maybe I could leverage my new bondmate to enlist his friend for fewer running laps or some shit.

When I was back on the training field, I whistled to get my team's attention and waited for them to fall in line while I went over my practice agenda for today. After adjusting my notes, I dropped my phone in my bag then went to stand in front of them.

"Where's Puck?"

Roko stretched his arms over his head, which distorted the sound of his voice. "He said he was called home for something. I didn't pry."

I squinted at him. "Tell him I'll be checking up on that." Puck had a habit of being called away and, more times than not, it was just him finding excuses to get out of training. "The rest of you, start with warm-up drills. Then you're doing elemental sparring."

"I thought we were doing shifting drills," Axel sneered.

"And now we're not." I glared back at him.

"Why?"

"Did you skip the long shower today, Axel? This isn't up for debate. Whatever your frustrations are, figure it out on your own time. Now get to work."

"What's the point of having us prepare for the next lesson if you're just going to change it?" he seethed, and the slack I'd given him ran out.

"What the fuck is your problem?" I walked up to him but restrained myself from punching his punk ass. Surprisingly, it was slightly less difficult than I expected, which was unusual for me. I definitely wanted to punch him for mouthing off, eyeing my girl, and acting like a prick. But there was another part of me that didn't want to hurt him.

Before today, we'd gotten along. He and Vale were the least annoying trainees I had, and more times than not, I found myself focused on their training and working longer with the two of them than any of the others.

I understood that draw to Vale now. Subconsciously, I wanted him to be the best so he could protect our mate when I wasn't around. But the connection to Axel I assumed was because he was my CI, and because of the obvious friendship they shared—one I thought I was getting in on. I didn't make friends easily and could count the few I had on three fingers—two of which were my brothers, and the other was Khade. Now that I was on the receiving end of Axel's bad attitude, I must have assumed too much and misunderstood.

"You are my problem. You're a fucking douche," he snarled like it was breaking news and he was the genius who'd cracked the case.

"And? That wasn't a problem three days ago," I snapped back. "What's different besides your attitude?"

"Things change." He glared at me.

"Well, whatever it is, keep it off my training field." I towered over him. "Or are we gonna—"

"You two are causing a scene." Vale slapped both of our backs at the same time, his ever-present smile on his face. Seriously, how could one guy be so happy all the fucking time?

"Tell that to your buddy." I jerked my chin at Axel, shrugging his hand off my shoulder.

Vale gave Axel his full attention and chuckled at him. "Are you uncomfortable in the bed you made again, Axe?"

"Fuck you." Axel turned his fury on his friend. "Why are you okay with this? You know what he's like," he sneered, flicking his eyes to me before focusing on Vale again.

"You lost any right to question anything," Vale whispered to him so low I knew I wasn't meant to hear it.

Neither the comment nor the anger made sense to me, but a burning curiosity lit up my chest. "What the hell are you two talking about?" I asked before I could think better of it.

"Nothing," they each said over the other.

I bristled at being left out of the conversation between them, but this was schoolyard shit, and I was done with it. "Both of you, get back into position. You're here to train, not fuck around."

Shoving my way between them, I shouted orders at the others and seethed while I corrected forms and stances. Vale playfully punched Axel a few times before Axel returned the jabs. They laughed at each other as they lined up, moving into a stretch routine before focusing on a core set.

"So, how was your walk with Honey?" Sidric, one of Vale's other buddies, asked mid sit-up.

I didn't know who he was talking about until Vale leaned over and punched him in the stomach. "I told you not to call her that anymore, asshole."

Sidric winced and coughed between laughs. "I told you it's just a nickname, dick. She's my friend, and I'm nosy."

My hackles raised once I realized they were talking about my mate. Glaring and growling down at Sidric, I had to clench my teeth and fists to stay in control of my temper. "What did you call her?"

"Calm down, hound. I know Lyra's your mate. I'm not a threat to you. I have a mate too." Sidric raised his hands at me. "We're all friends here."

"Well, most of us." Brev side-eyed Axel from his plank position, but I couldn't make sense of it either. They'd all shown similar dislike and dismissal of Axel and only seemed to tolerate his presence when Vale was with them.

"I don't know you. We're not friends. Don't call my mate endearments, or I'll break your face."

"Dude, chill." Sidric still had his hands up, but he was smirking. I had half a mind to smack it off.

"He's harmless," Vale grunted between push-ups. "He's yanking your chain. Don't take the bait."

"You mated types are so uptight." Brev looked around, lounging instead of working out. "You get jealous over the dumbest shit."

"Your day's coming." Sidric swept his arms out from where he was leaning on them and laughed when Brev bounced his head off the turf.

"So?" Vale peered up at me with that full grin again. "How was your walk? Does our dorm meet your approval?"

I wasn't discussing anything in front of all these guys. So, I added a weight between his shoulder blades and whistled at them through my fingers. "One more word out of any of you, and you're running laps with a resistance load for the rest of the day."

Chapter Twenty-Three

Vale was dressed and waiting for us at the kitchen table the following morning when Khade and I arrived through the portal from the cabin.

"Good morning." I kissed him on the cheek before stealing his coffee.

"How was your night?" He pulled me onto his lap and nibbled at my neck.

I didn't answer and instead batted my lashes at him as I sipped his drink.

"How was training?" Khade pulled out a chair and sat with his own mug. "Did Rhett ease up on your training or make you work harder?" He gave Vale a knowing smirk.

"Like you need to ask. I thought he was a hard-ass before. Now, he's an absolute nightmare." Vale grumbled. "I haven't been sore like this since I first started shifting."

"Good." Khade nodded in approval. "He'll make you the best. That's what Lyra deserves."

Vale looked at me with a grin. "Of course she does."

"And the others? How were they?"

"Great." Vale took his coffee back and gulped half. "Except Axel. He had a bad night." Vale chortled.

I shifted to look at him better. "Why? I thought they got along?"

Vale shrugged. “They did until yesterday.”

“What was said?” Khade asked.

“Axel asked me if I was comfortable with Rhett and said, ‘You know what he’s like’. Which could mean any number of things. Rhett has a reputation.” He flicked his eyes to me, sounding uncomfortable bringing it up. “He’s also a hard-ass and a hothead sometimes.”

“He’s a good man.” Khade held my gaze. “I’m happy for you both.”

“You don’t have a problem with him, then?” Vale asked. “You’re kind of a possessive control freak too; I thought you might be pissed.”

Khade smirked. “Not even a little.”

“And you?” I turned to Vale. “Do you have a problem with him?”

I hadn’t known to be worried about this until this conversation. What if my mates didn’t like each other? How would that even work?

“No, my sweet mate. I don’t have a problem with him.” He leaned forward and gave me a quick kiss. “I like him. As long as he stops adding weights to my workouts, we’ll get along just fine.” He smirked.

“And if he doesn’t?”

“I’ll put his hand in warm water while he sleeps.” He gave me his bright smile, teeth and all, which made me chuckle at his teasing. “Speaking of, we should go. Your breakfast date will be waiting.”

“I thought he was coming here?” My brows pinched as I looked at the time.

“Nah, I told him I’d walk you to the gates. I have a meeting with the coach to talk about my position on the Starball team next season.”

With that announcement, it was my turn to give him a big, toothy smile. “I want a jersey with your name and number on it.”

“Damn right.” Vale stood, flipped me over his shoulder, and gave my ass a playful tap.

Khade kissed me goodbye when I was on my feet again, then Vale and I left our dorm.

“You look well-rested.” Rhett’s deep voice greeted Vale when we approached.

“Sleeping next to Lyra will do that.” Vale’s chest puffed out as he boasted.

I didn't know if I should laugh or be mortified at the insinuation. So I settled on a combination of the two and blushed. "Stop teasing."

"I'm bragging. I get to do that when I have the perfect mate." He lifted me and kissed my lips. "Plus, it's nice to have something over Rhett. He's been running my ass into the ground for weeks. This seems fair." He winked at me.

"I'm alright with a little riffing, sugar," Rhett drawled, holding out his hand for me to take. "Besides, Vale's stuck with me as his trainer, and once I make you mine, I'll outperform him in more ways than one," he implied with a swagger, making my blush darken.

The three mates I already had were full alpha-male testosterone—how was I ever going to add a fourth and keep up?

Vale chuckled at my embarrassment and kissed my cheeks right where they felt the most heated. "I'm so glad you picked me first so I could watch you find the rest of your mates from my front-row seat."

"You're incorrigible."

Vale held out his hand to Rhett to shake. "Go feed our Lyra. She's only had coffee this morning. She likes sweet and savory; blueberries are her favorite, and she'll never say no to anything with hollandaise."

"Got it. I'll take good care of her." Rhett grinned down at me. "And I know the perfect place."

"I'll see you later," Vale called over his shoulder.

"Don't wait up," Rhett hollered as Vale's booming laughter echoed across the quad.

Walking with Rhett was just as I'd expected after the night before, but the cover of darkness had made people braver than they were in the harsh light of day. While we received a few questioning looks from those who noticed our clasped hands, there were plenty more who were just focused on getting his attention. Like last night, though, Rhett kept his focus on me, allowing me to ignore them too.

When we were seated at a corner table on a balcony-top restaurant, we continued our casual conversation from the walk over. We covered all the bases: favorite foods, drinks, places to go, books, and movies, and had moved onto career choices and studies for me. I told him in broad terms about my business degree decision.

"I'm only in my first year, so I'm not certain how it will be applicable to what I end up doing," I told him honestly and vaguely.

It was easier for me to ask him about specific parts of his job since I knew him through Vale. He couldn't tell me much because it was classified, which I should have expected him to say, but it was odd for me to hear all the same. I changed the topic after that so we wouldn't feel awkward about it when I revealed to him. He asked me about my family, so I glazed over my family tree, giving him the same general answers I did when I met everyone for the first time. I had to stick to my story of only having three siblings since that's what was decided when I first went to Araphel. I didn't mention any jobs or mates my brothers had, though, since it was likely he'd met all of them at one point. It was a long shot that he'd draw parallels, but just in case, I stuck to basic facts and nothing too personal. If he noticed, he didn't mention it or seem to mind.

"You're a triplet?" My mouth gaped at the news. "And all three of you are Sidhe Hounds? That's kind of amazing." I couldn't help it and instantly wondered if multiples were in our future. With him being a triplet and Khade's father being a twin, the chances were high.

"It was a challenge growing up." He smiled at my enthusiasm. "They're both in the guard too. Walker works intelligence, and Hayes is a strategist."

"Your parents must be proud. Did you follow in their footsteps, or did you all just have the same drive?"

He huffed out a humorless laugh. "That's too much story to get into now, sugar, but no. Mom was an artist, and my father runs the family business, Irondale Mining." He didn't sound impressed by this fact, but the business was well-known and played an important part in supplying materials for the entire Night Kingdom.

"I guess that's why your name sounded familiar." I grinned. "You didn't want to go into the family business?"

"Hell no. Dad led us down a different path. He might expect it someday, but..." He let the sentence drop and shook his head.

"What does your mom do now? You said she was an artist; she's not anymore?" I asked after we placed our orders.

"She still is, just not the way she used to be before us." His smile was soft. "She experienced complications during childbirth and requires assistance with many things now. It affected her motor skills, but when she's having a good day, she'll put paint to canvas. I can't wait to tell her about you. She'll be over the moon."

"I'm looking forward to it." The way he looked when he spoke about her filled my heart and softened his tough exterior he showed to the world.

We were halfway through breakfast when Dina from my elemental class sauntered up to the table. "Hey, Lyra." She greeted me like we were old friends, then winked and held up a piece of paper between her fingers. "I didn't know you were friends with the captain," she said conversationally, then put the paper on the table and slid it to Rhett.

He lifted the edge for a quick peek, then slid it back to her. "Lyra is my mate."

She smiled at me, then jerked her head back and forth between us like her brain was short-circuiting, her face contorting as she stammered and stumbled. "Oh... oh... OH my goddess! I'm sorry. I didn't know. I thought he was single. Oh my—"

"It's fine." I put my hands up to calm her down. "We found each other yesterday. You didn't know."

She nodded vigorously while I spoke, flicking her eyes to Rhett then right back to me as if she would get in trouble for simply looking at him. "I'm so sorry. I never would have come over here if I knew..."

"I know." I smiled at her. "I don't blame you; he's hot."

Dina blushed and gave me a shy smile. "Thank you. I don't know why people were such a bitch to you when you first got here. You're super nice."

I blurted out a laugh. "Thanks, I guess."

Rhett's brows drew down at the comment, but he looked up at Dina instead of questioning me about it. "I would appreciate it if you spread the word. I'd like to avoid interactions like this in the future." Rhett's bass tone seemed to vibrate the air around us.

Dina's eyes widened at the sound of his voice as she slowly nodded at him. "Of course. Absolutely. I'm so sorry." Her voice was high-pitched, then she jerked her head back to look at me. "I'll see you in class, Lyra." She waved awkwardly at me like we weren't just a foot away from each other, then hurriedly left our table.

I watched her, but instead of sitting back down with her friends, she whispered to them, grabbed her purse, and left.

"Hopefully, that will help," he grumbled and stabbed the sausage on his plate. "I'm thinking of enlisting Vale's friend, Puck, too."

My smile widened at the mention of my brother's name. "Oh?"

"I don't know how well you know him, but he's a gossip. He'll spread the word." He spoke around a mouthful, then chugged half of his water. "I don't want to be an asshole, but I will if this shit doesn't stop."

"When Vale and I revealed, it only took a day or two for people to realize. Word will get around." I reached out and put my hand on his. "Don't make a fuss on my account."

He shrugged, but I didn't get the sense that it was for me; rather, he didn't care if he came across as brash to others and would do it anyway if the propositioning continued.

"What did she mean about people being mean to you?" His brows drew together.

I shook my head and cut into my pancake. "I had a slow start making friends when I first arrived. It's all good now."

He was quiet for a moment before he said, "If anyone's bothering you, I want you to tell me."

"Of course." I smiled at him. "So, did you ever date anyone?"

He coughed on his drink at the question. "Uh, no... I mean, not really. Are you sure you want to talk about this?"

"We had lives before we met. I don't want details, but in general, I'm curious. You draw a lot of attention to yourself," I teased, wondering if this was what it would have been like with Khade if we could have been public with our relationship.

He set his fork down, then scratched the back of his head before answering. "When I was younger, around your age, I had a few friends with benefits." He drummed his fingers on the table. "Nothing serious enough to call it dating, though."

"Same." I nodded. "Well, unless you count Sidric."

"Sidric?" His voice was slightly louder with widening eyes. "From my training class?"

"Yes." I held back my smile at his reaction. "We met shortly after I arrived at Araphel and had a fling until I met Vale. Are you okay?"

He was as still as a statue, staring at me intently. "Does Vale know?" He looked confused.

"Of course."

He nodded slowly, then shook his head. "That's why Vale told him to stop calling you— Why does he call you honey?"

I blurted out a laugh. "Is he still doing that?"

"Vale tells him to stop, but it seems more like a game between them." He relaxed in his chair again and crossed his huge arms over his chest. "What's the story there? Or is it just some random moniker he termed for you? You don't have to tell me, but I am curious."

"It's not a secret. I'll tell you anything you want to know." I dabbed the corners of my mouth with my napkin and put it on my plate so the server could clear the table. "I have a bee allergy that includes honey. For whatever reason, Sidric decided to call me honey after that." I shrugged. "It's nothing special, more of a fun, teasing nickname than anything else."

After breakfast, we decided to go for a walk in the forest by Araphel. There were nice trails and even some picnic and outdoor gaming areas, but we stuck to the manicured walkways and dirt paths. We passed a small lake, where people were soaking up the sun in both their fae and shifted forms. Rhett even caught a wayward frisbee, and when he threw it back, a griffin snatched it out of the air, which turned into a game of chase with some others taking flight after him.

"Any other medical considerations I should know?" he asked after steering us away from a patch of wildflowers. "Peanuts? Shellfish? Animals?"

"No. Just bees and honey," I told him, then went on to explain my jewelry, and Callie and Jed's project.

He was very interested and wanted to be updated with their progress. He even asked if he could join me next time to talk to them about their work and look at the nulliflies they'd created.

I was glad I could do this for Rhett since Khade was frustrated about being excluded, especially given that having Vale there wasn't enough to ease his concerns. Maybe now, with two mates involved, Khade wouldn't be so wary about their testing on me.

He was quiet for a few minutes, and I thought we were just enjoying a peaceful walk together until he led me to a more secluded clearing and turned to face me. "Earlier, when we were discussing my work, I mentioned I couldn't say much about it. That's still true. But part of what I do involves intelligence—collecting data, analyzing information for threats. It's impossible for me to shut that part of my brain off."

I nodded but wasn't sure how to respond to this or why he was saying it, so I waited.

"I have no reason not to trust you or Vale, but I get the distinct sense that you're both hiding something." My eyes widened, but he continued before I could respond. "Vale seems to be the only one who tolerates Axel in our training group. Your friends, including Sidric, can hardly stand him. I never had a problem with Axel until we were revealed as mates, and now Axel seems to have taken issue with me. Given their behaviors and comments, and what you've mentioned, I have to ask again—was there anything between you and Axel? You were open about your past with Sidric, and as you said, we all have a history. If not a relationship, is there something else between you two that I should know about?"

"Yes." I didn't bother to dodge the pointed question. He was asking and deserved an honest answer. "I will tell you everything, but I need to send a message first." I opened my group chat to Vale and Khade and sent them a message about what was happening.

"Okay." His brows pulled down. "You're safe with me, regardless of what you have to say."

I smiled up at him. "I didn't think I wasn't. I am letting Vale know, though. It was upsetting for him to hear when he found out and wanted to be informed when the time came for you and me to have this conversation."

"Understood." His face turned into a scowl, and he pulled out his phone, tapping hard on the screen, then shoved it in his back pocket again.

After pinging my location and sending it to them, I put my phone away, raised a privacy shield around us, and squared my shoulders.

"How much do you know about the rumors surrounding last season's spring revelry?"

He didn't take it well. Actually, that was an understatement.

After I finished telling him everything I could without revealing to him who I truly was, he began to visibly shake. He was grinding his teeth, repeatedly balling his hands into fists, and breathing heavily. When I stepped forward to comfort him, he jerked his head no.

"I don't trust myself right now." The words were said through clenched teeth, punctuating his statement with a deliberate step back from me. "I'm sorry." He panted heavily, then spun around and pounded his fist into a tree until the trunk cracked. Broken pieces of bark and blood splattered his shirt and face, followed by a beastly growl that sent birds flying and silenced the insects before he exploded into his shifted form.

In front of me, where Rhett had been seconds ago, was now a massive Sidhe Hound, growling and twitching as if trying to shake off the rage.

"Rhett?"

He turned his head to look at me, his eyes glowing red, glaring, with his snout wrinkled and his lips pulled back to reveal sharp teeth. He chuffed and dropped his head before he began to pace. Each pass brought him closer until he was circling me.

Just when I thought he was calming down, his head jerked up, his ears twitched, and in an instant, I wasn't surrounded by just one angry hound but three. Rhett's form had trembled before he'd split into two more equally formidable versions of himself.

The pitch-black hounds were enormous, muscular beasts. Their features were boxy and wide like a lion, but sharp and threatening like a dragon. They had large teeth, long snouts, and severe eyes. Their fur was so short it was barely there, revealing the brawny muscles that flexed and contracted beneath their flesh. A row of short spikes ran down their spines to the tips of their tails, which cracked like whips as they twitched in the air. Powerful legs ended in paws with dragon claws that raked the earth, leaving grooves behind in their agitation. The ground beneath my feet vibrated with their constant growling and patrol as they continued their circuit around me.

I wasn't scared for my safety. I felt the opposite—protected from the world and everything bad and dangerous in it with him as my defense. I was, however, worried about what had set him off to keep him this way.

Vale's dragon roared from above before he swooped down to land hard next to us, but Rhett didn't react to him. Instead, he turned his fiery gaze in the opposite direction to where Khade's Beithir had appeared and was reared back, glaring down at him. Khade's cobra hood was wide, his teeth were exposed, and he was hissing menacingly at the three Sidhe Hounds.

Any attempts I made to speak or calm them down were drowned out by the persistent rumbling until finally Khade lowered himself from his towering position and transformed.

"Rhett." He held up his hands. "I am not a threat to you. You sent for me. Let Vale take your mate home."

Rhett looked at me and watched as Vale moved close enough to hook his wing talon around my waist. He huffed and dropped his head like a nod before the three of him made room, moving to line up and face Khade. Then his hackles raised, he dropped his stance into a defensive position, and roared at the gray wolf that barreled through the trees.

"No!" Khade yelled and held up his hand, but it was too late. Rhett's forms charged after Axel's wolf, who in turn growled and leaped at the hound in the center of the three. "Get her out of here!" Khade hollered at Vale, who had already grabbed me with his forelimb and was lifting off.

I tried to argue, but my voice was lost in the cacophony of their snarling. Unable to shift or focus my magic, all I could do was watch as Khade shifted once more and hurled himself into the brawl between my newest mate, who wanted me, and the one who had rejected me.

Chapter Twenty-Four

Vale took me straight home, where I stomped around the dorm in a fit of annoyance and anger, to the point of tears. None of them were responding to text messages or picking up phone calls. I was confused, didn't know what was going on, and worried.

"Will you please go check on them?" I asked Vale for the umpteenth time. I had opened all the sliding doors and was pacing the floor as I watched the forest.

"I'm not leaving you." He rubbed my shoulders. "They will be fine. I promise." He kissed the top of my head before pulling me against his back, holding me in a tight hug.

We stood like that long enough that my feet started hurting and my stomach growled in hunger. Thankfully, we had leftover mac 'n' cheese we'd loaded up on from the dining hall, so I didn't have to think too hard about what to eat.

As the sun began to set and there was still no word from any of them, I started to pace again. I took a shower to try to distract myself and, finally, after I was dressed in my pajamas, I sensed Rhett when he crossed the protection spell.

Vale had his arms crossed over his chest as he looked Rhett over, shaking his head while failing to hold back a smirk. "Feel better?"

"No," Rhett grunted, then turned to look at me when I stepped out onto the porch next to them. His features contorted before tensing. "I can explain."

"I should hope so."

"I'll be inside if you need anything," Vale told me and gave Rhett a quick nod before leaving us alone.

"How badly did you hurt him?" I bit the inside of my cheek as I waited for him to answer, worried about what he'd say.

Rhett held my eyes for a moment, then dropped his head in his hands to scrub his palms against his scalp before answering me. "He held his own. But I'm glad I called for backup. Khade is a friend of mine. We trained together in the guard, and we have a close working and personal relationship. I would have taken it too far if he hadn't been there. I'm sorry I scared you. I'm embarrassed and ashamed, but..." He took my hand. "I'm struggling with myself right now, Lyra, and I can't fully explain why."

Because of the geas and the restrictions we were both bound by, I thought I understood his dilemma, but I needed to be certain. "Can you try?"

"Part of me—the part that is your mate—knows what I did was right in defending you and our bond. I don't know if I could have even stopped myself. You may not agree, but I don't regret it. He broke something sacred."

"Violence isn't the answer."

"Not always." He nodded. "But sometimes it's necessary. Maybe not in this instance, but I can't take it back, and I don't know if I would."

"And the other part of you? The part that isn't my mate?"

"Didn't have all the information, overreacted, and could have put something very important in jeopardy if I hadn't called ahead and brought in Khade. I'll have to answer for that in front of my COs, and likely the Queen and the Knight Lords."

"Rhett." I reached out for him, surprised by the potential reprimand.

"I assaulted a recruit. Regardless of the reasons why, I shouldn't have. I'm a trained professional, and it's my job to protect people, even those I don't agree with or who are in the wrong."

"Will you lose your position?" I didn't think so, and if I could do anything to help him, I would.

"No." He shook his head. "I messed up, but the extenuating circumstances work in my favor. I'm only worried about how you see me now and if you can forgive me."

Thinking back to when Vale had come to me after doing the same thing to Axel when he first learned the truth, I reasoned that if I could have forgiven Vale so easily, then why not Rhett? I'd always said I wouldn't moderate their relationships. Axel's rejection of me, and subsequently our bond, affected them too. They were entitled to their feelings, and I wouldn't—couldn't—control how they felt or reacted about it. They needed to process everything in their own way, even if that meant doing something that I didn't like or agree with.

"I understand why you're angry. I think there's more to Axel's story, and I believe he regrets his decision. While I don't know for certain why he did what he did, I've chosen to forgive him. I don't expect you to, but I don't want to live in anger. I can forgive you, but I don't want there to be a next time."

"I don't make promises I can't keep," he told me seriously. "I'll need time. I'm still required to train him, and it might prove difficult for me, but I will try to keep a level head. If for no other reason, I want to be better for you. You deserve nothing less than my best, and I promise you will get it." He lifted my hand and kissed my knuckles.

"We're okay, Rhett. I promise."

He closed his eyes and let out a heavy sigh. "Thank you."

Rhett left not long after that, and while I felt better having talked it over with him, I was still worried about Axel. I asked Vale to reach out to him, but he was met with silence, which only added to my frustration.

Eventually, we left the dorm to meet Khade at the cabin, where we talked over everything that Rhett didn't know we could discuss.

"It's not my place to speak on his anger and his shifting, but when he's ready to talk about it, I know he will with you," Khade told me vaguely. "In the meantime, he was made aware of our suspicions. Previously, we'd only told Rhett that Axel was going to be his informant and didn't go into too much detail. Now, he knows there's a high probability that Axel is under a geas and was potentially forced into his actions. Actions that may or may not include his rejection of you. It was the only thing that finally calmed him down."

"How was Axel?" My voice was quieter than I'd meant it to be, and I was trying really hard not to be emotional, but I didn't think I fooled either of them.

Khade pulled me against him. "Rhett is very good at his job, and that reason is why he was chosen to train Vale and the others. It's because of Rhett's training that Axel was able to walk away. He will be fine," he told me and left it at that.

I tossed and turned between them for a while until I eventually fell asleep, or at least was exhausted enough to slip into the ether.

The silence was as loud as the room was dark. I knew, physically, that I was still with Vale and Khade in the cabin, but my spirit was elsewhere. A lamp flickered on to life outside of the window, giving off enough light to cast a glow into the room and make me aware of the other person who lingered here. Which was what it seemed like—that Axel was lingering, hiding away in the dark.

The room was a chaotic mess: books and scrolls stacked and open, scattered across his desk; there were ancient tomes about spell work, rites, and history books I recognized regarding the first queen and her ascension.

There was a faint rattle on the side table where his phone sat, and after he checked it, he stood and paced the floor as if agitated. He mumbled to himself, but I couldn't quite make out the words. His presence was as palpable as the pain pulsing in the solitude of his room. Frustration hung heavy in the air, and the anger swirling in the space felt dark and dangerous. If it could have reached its focus, the target undoubtedly wouldn't have survived its wrath.

When Axel's rambling came to an end, he sighed, then lifted a glass, which brought my attention to the sharp angle of his bruised jaw. The liquid glistened as it caught the light, then disappeared in one hard gulp. Wiping his mouth on his sleeve, he clenched his teeth before sailing the tumbler across the room, shattering it against the wall and scattering shards across the floor. Shoving his hands into his hair, he tugged at the locks and cursed at himself before bellowing into the isolation he assumed surrounded him. A rush of breathtaking agony suffocated the room as the shattered remains of our bond throbbed between us.

His anguish was so recognizable that it drove me closer to him, overwhelmed by the need to fix what was broken.

With my proximity, he exhaled, and his shoulders relaxed as some of the tension visibly left his body. Slipping his hand into his pocket, he pulled out a white strip of fabric before sitting in the chair.

When I knelt before him, he whispered softly to the room again. His eyes were unfocused and dilated, but he wasn't frantic this time, and I understood what he was saying.

"I'm so sorry." His throat bobbed as he lifted the swatch to his nose before shoving it back in his pocket.

I followed him when he left the room.

He took an unfamiliar path that led through the quad outside of the dorms. As we walked by students milling about, they ignored him as if they couldn't see him, even when we came within inches of their presence.

When we reached a set of travel portals, we stepped through one, then another, until we arrived in an empty room in a grand estate. I followed him down a hallway, walking behind him and noticing for the first time the tuxedo he was wearing. Echoes of voices and music bounced off the walls, accompanied by laughter and the clinking of glasses.

The room we came to was teeming with guests, all dressed in formal wear. Tables of hors d'oeuvres sat around the opulent space, champagne towers flowed, and flowers adorned the walls. I recognized several faces in the room, but many were strangers to me. Still, I took the opportunity to scan each one and commit them to memory. I also made a mental note of the cloaked figures whose faces were hidden from view but held a prominent place in the room.

They were all happily celebrating the gathering they attended, carefree in their fete and conversation, brazen in their association with a potential traitor to the crown.

When we reached the crowded banquet hall, a hushed whisper settled over the room as Axel walked through the entrance.

"Ah, there he is now." Azael turned to look at Axel, freezing me momentarily as I worried if he'd see me. But his eyes never wavered from his son's and instead seemed to root Axel into place.

Azael held out an arm in welcome, and when Axel didn't move immediately to join him, admonishment passed over Azael's features. His lips moved nearly imperceptibly as a string of silent words, not meant for other ears, passed between them.

When Axel hesitantly moved to stand by his side, Azael's mask slipped back on as he turned and beamed at the crowd. "Ladies and gentlemen, tonight marks an extraordinary night for our movement. In the approaching days, we will make our grand appearance and take our cause to the public." His announcement was met with grandiloquent cheers, raised glasses, and light claps.

Their egotism was as evident as their ingratiation of the host. The idea that any movement could amass a following with such selfish behavior at its core was astonishing to me.

"Magic is a powerful and immutable gift with which we are fortunate to be endowed. But with its constancy comes limitations," he praised before feigning somberness. "Unfortunately, our cause to restore our kingdoms to their rightful rulers faces the obstacle known as the Queen and her bonds. As such, their connection to the land and the power they share cannot be broken, but we do not need it to be. With your support and the backing of our people, we can return to better days. My friends, we do not seek to completely overturn the current rule. Instead, we aim to match their strength to confront it head-on."

Azael straightened his back and lifted his chin a fraction as he scanned the room, basking in the undivided attention he had while his ego surely grew.

"Esteemed guests, please welcome our returning Kings of Summer, Autumn, and Winter." He held out his hand again, this time in the direction of two doors facing opposite of him. The ornate barriers opened simultaneously, revealing three fae males standing shoulder to shoulder, dressed in full regalia.

The guests greeted them with bows and curtsies. And when their sons were introduced, followed by their mates and daughters, they were also met with deference.

My disbelief was at war with my anger at what I was witnessing, and if there had ever been a doubt these people were traitors to my mother, it was undeniable now.

"Last, but certainly not least, please welcome the former nominal regent of the Spring Court, Irvine ." As a second set of doors opened, the guests' attention shifted to another side of the room, where he praised the older male.

Glenleaf was greeted with less deference than the others but received plenty of reverent respect typical of a high-ranking councilman. When he took his place next to Azael, I noticed how similarly they were dressed.

It was when his mate and daughter were introduced, though, that I suddenly got answers to the many questions I'd had since first arriving at Araphel. Jana walked in the room with an heir of importance that rivaled Azael's. After she curtsied each of the fraudulent kings, she placed herself beside Axel.

At her proximity, an all-consuming rage coursed through me—a feeling I'd only experienced once before—with disgust and abhorrence vying for second place. A knot formed in my stomach as anxiety and dread tightened my chest, making it hard for me to breathe. An overwhelming urge to leave the gala left my hands shaking, but I couldn't go—despite wanting to, I simply *couldn't* leave.

And in this moment, I knew with absolute clarity that these emotions were not my own, but that I was sharing them with Axel—an experience I'd had many times before, but one I hadn't understood until now.

"Irvine, though reluctant to embrace the responsibility of rule, has pledged his support to me," Azael's voice boomed over the crowd. He rested his hand on Irvine's shoulder and scanned the room before turning his gaze to Axel. "In the absence of a male heir, he has entrusted my family with the responsibility of inheriting the Spring Court, ensuring continuity in our lineage," he bragged, announcing himself as king of the fourth season. "Each of us has been tasked to bring balance to our rule, equal to that of the Queen's reign. To ensure mutual trust and solidify our alliance, we will reinforce our bonds and fortify our new order by reinstating covenant marriage—a pledge bound by magic and as unbreakable as a fated bond itself. In doing so, we guarantee not only our unity and strength but also the prosperity and stability for all. This is our pledge to the future, an oath and commitment we make to this alliance, and tonight, a vow that my family will lead by example. Ladies and gentlemen, I am proud to announce the engagement of my son, Axel, to the lovely noble daughter and nominal Spring Court heiress, Jana Glenleaf."

My hearing dulled as the room cheered with the announcement of their union.

My chest felt like it had been ripped open. I struggled to breathe as I stumbled back.

The room went fuzzy around the edges as my eyes blurred with unshed tears, and a sob ripped through my lips.

Axel turned, his face gaunt and emotionless, until his eyes met mine, then his expression dropped. He reached out as if to touch me, grief marring his features as he cried out in panic, "No!"

But everything went black as darkness swept over me.

Readers Note

Thank you for reading Summer Knights Dream! Your support means the world, and I look forward to sharing the rest of Lyra's story with you.

For the latest updates and news, be sure to follow me on social media at www.ariadnebreylard.com

Happy reading!

Ariadne

Acknowledgements

I extend my deepest gratitude to my incredible husband. Your unwavering support and encouragement have been my anchor throughout this literary adventure. Your belief in me has been invaluable, and I truly couldn't be more grateful for the constant strength you've provided.

To my children, your patience and understanding during late nights and the writing process have not gone unnoticed. You are my greatest creation. I love you to the farthest star and all the way back—times infinity.

To my beta readers, thank you for pointing out insights and offering constructive feedback, helping me see what I couldn't. To my street team, your passion for the characters and the story is beyond appreciated.

To the fans, your unwavering enthusiasm has made this journey all the more rewarding.

To the talented artists and diligent editors whose expertise has elevated the quality of this book.

I am sincerely grateful for each one of you.

Thank you,

Ariadne

Night Kingdom

Queen Hesper Araphel

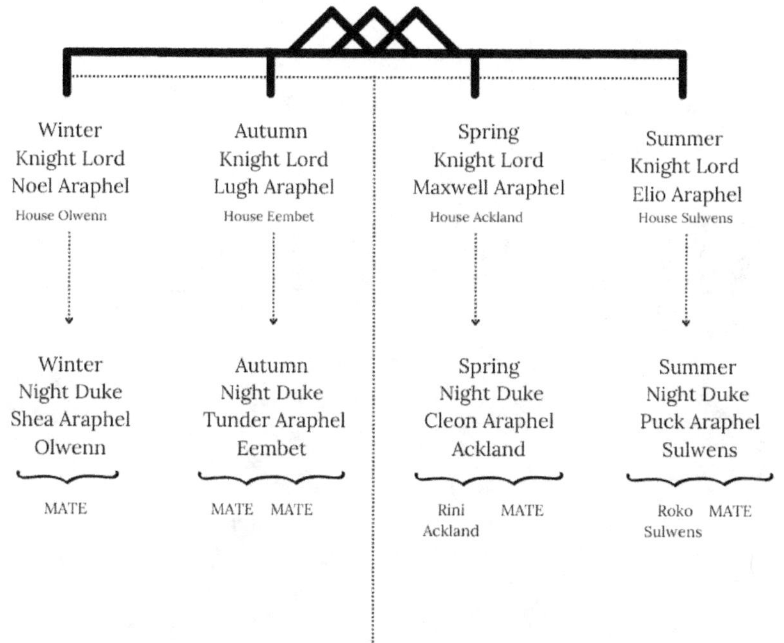

Princess Lyra Araphel

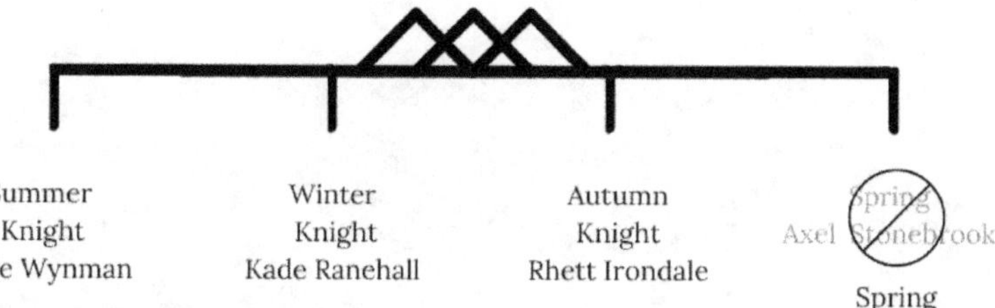

- Lyra (*Leer-uh*) — Night Princess of the Night Kingdom
- Vale Wynman (*WIN-mən*) — Lyra's Summer Mate, Noble Son, Wynman House
- Khade Ranehall (RAYN-*hall*) — Lyra's Winter Mate, Night Court's Counsel, Ranehall House
- Rhett Irondale — Lyra's Autumn Mate, Night Guard, Captain, Irondale House
- Mother — Hesper — Queen of the Night Kingdom
- Father — Noel (NoUL) — Knight Lord of the Night Kingdom, from Winter Court
- Pai — Elio (*Eh-lee-oh*) — Knight Lord of the Night Kingdom, from Summer Court
- Baba— Lugh (LOO) — Knight Lord of the Night Kingdom, from Autumn Court
- Papa— Maxwell — Knight Lord of the Night Kingdom, from Spring Court
- Puck — Lyra's older brother, Night Duke of the Night Kingdom, Summer, Elio's son
- Shea — Lyra's older brother, Night Duke of the Night Kingdom, Winter, Noel's son
- Tunder — Lyra's older brother, Night Duke of the Night Kingdom, Spring, Maxwell's son
- Cleon — Lyra's older brother, Night Duke of the Night Kingdom, Autumn, Lugh's son
- High Priestess — Prophetess of Fate, Knight Kingdom
- Axel Stonebrook — Spring Court Noble, rejected Lyra
- Roko (*Rock-oh*) — Puck's mate
- Callie — Summer Court, Lyra's best friend
- Professor Atticus Warrock — Economics Professor
- Jana Glenleaf— Axel's ex-girlfriend, Spring Court Noble
- Jed — Lyra's friend
- Brev — Lyra's friend
- Sidric — Lyra's friend
- Professor Ivy Rootsworth — Earth Elemental Professor
- Professor Reginald Copperplate — Accounting Professor
- Azael Stonebrook (AH-zay-el) — Axel's father, Spring Court Noble, Councilman Stonebrook
- Irvine Glenleaf— Jana's father, Spring Court Noble, Councilman
- Caldor — Enchantment Specialist
- Atlas — Callie's mate
- Elle — Callie's mate
- Dina — Student in Lyra's class

About the author

Ariadne Breylard is an author with a passion for crafting fantasy romance novels that are both sweet and spicy. She resides in a beautiful mountainous region, where the natural surroundings provide endless inspiration for her writing.

With an infectious imagination and a love for all things fantastical, Ariadne weaves tales of epic love stories, enchanting worlds, and mythical creatures that leave readers spellbound.

Her captivating writing style has gained her a dedicated following of readers and won the hearts of fans worldwide, putting her books at the top of Amazon Best Seller Lists.

When she's not writing, Ariadne can be found tending to her garden, filled with an array of vibrant flowers and plants. She also enjoys spending time with her family, beloved animals, and listening to the enchanting melodies of neoclassical compositions.

If you enjoyed Ariadne Breylard's writing, explore more worlds crafted under the author's other pen names.

NVREADS.COM/NVP-PENNAMES

www.ingramcontent.com/pod-product-compliance
Lightning Source LLC
LaVergne TN
LVHW010652110826
845149LV00014B/3052